This time there was no condemning stab of conscience when she did not struggle.

Louisa recalled his first kiss too vividly to expect that she could or should do other than melt into his embrace. This second venture was even longer in duration and far more ardent. "Oh, I do love you," a voice breathed at its conclusion, and she realized with a wave of sadness that the voice was hers.

"Do you?" Lord Lyston answered huskily, tenderly pushing the hair back from her cheek while he held her close and gazed at her. "My God, Louisa, you're beautiful. I can't get my fill of looking at you. Lord knows, no other woman has ever had this effect on me."

Also by Marian Devon
Published by Fawcett Books:

MISS ARMSTEAD WEARS BLACK GLOVES
MISS ROMNEY FLIES TOO HIGH
M'LADY RIDES FOR A FALL
SCANDAL BROTH
SIR SHAM
A QUESTION OF CLASS
ESCAPADE
FORTUNES OF THE HEART
MISS OSBORNE MISBEHAVES
LADY HARRIET TAKES CHARGE
MISTLETOE AND FOLLY
A SEASON FOR SCANDAL
A HEART ON HIS SLEEVE
AN UNCIVIL SERVANT

DEFIANT MISTRESS

Marian Devon

FAWCETT CREST • NEW YORK

A Fawcett Crest Book
Published by Ballantine Books
Copyright © 1983 by Anne Devon

All rights reserved under International and Pan-American Copyright Conventions. Published in the United States of America by Ballantine Books, a division of Random House, Inc., New York, and simultaneously in Canada by Random House of Canada Limited, Toronto.

Library of Congress Catalog Card Number: 94-94032

ISBN 0-449-21667-5

This edition published by arrangement with The Berkley/Jove Publishing Group.

Manufactured in the United States of America

First Edition: June 1994

10 9 8 7 6 5 4 3 2 1

Chapter One

"FOR GAWD'S SAKE, GET ON WITH IT! SMOTHER THE fat old cow!"

The shout from the pit was punctuated with a rotten orange that splatted on stage between Desdemona and Othello, speckling them both with stinking pulp. Another fruit, not so well directed, landed near the wings. The actress waiting there for her cue was spared a similar messy fate by the quick intervention of a British lieutenant who snatched her out of range. "That damned well did it," he growled between clenched teeth. "Get your things, Louisa. I'm taking you out of here."

"Don't be silly," the young woman said, inching closer to the curtain. "Sssssh—I'll miss my cue."

Onstage, for the only time that evening, the leading lady got an emotion right. Unfortunately, the naked fear that she projected was not for the Moor, who at scene's end would take her life—it was for the audience, who might beat Othello to it.

The house was packed from gallery to pit. The best of theater companies would have been at pains to hold the unruly audience. This third-rate touring troop treading the boards of Brussels' seediest opera house had no hope at all. There was too much real drama outside the theater for costume, makeup, scenery, and properties to rival it. The make-believe of actors could not take the minds of the audience from the parts they themselves had been cast to play.

The spectators were mainly English military, the theater a Red Sea of uniforms, from the three-tiered balcony to the benches in the pit, its crimson only occasionally interspersed by yellows, blues, pinks, whites, and other colors worn by female camp followers come out from home or recruited from the Belgian population.

The real spoiler of the evening was Napoleon Bonaparte. He was far more to blame for the unruliness of the audience than was the inept Desdemona, chief target of the noisy critics. For the Corsican had broken out of exile and raised an army of his disbanded veterans. Now he was on the move, while the English and Prussian armies awaited him in Belgium. In a matter of days, the clash would come. In the meantime, on with the show! Only this show was impossible. And the audience had let it be known with jeers, catcalls, and whistles, topped off by an occasional pelting of fruit.

"What, not a whore?" Othello shouted over all the hubbub. The young thespian in the wings took a deep breath and prepared to enter.

"Don't do it, Louisa. That crowd's ready to take the place apart. They're foxed, the whole lot of 'em. Any minute now, they'll storm the stage."

"Well, they haven't turned on me yet." She

crossed her fingers, and, while the mad Moor ranted, "You, mistress, that have the office opposite to Saint Peter and keep the gates of hell!" she strode onstage to thunderous applause. It soon became apparent, even to the disgruntled Lieutenant Grayson, that no matter how much the audience hated Desdemona, they loved Emilia more. Indeed, the only thing that had prevented them from running riot and closing down the show was the frequent appearance of this newcomer in her secondary role. But they had let it be known in loud and frequent shouts that a terrible injustice in casting had been done. "Smother the fat old cow and take her maid to bed!"

And it was true that the ingenue seemed made to order for the leading role. Hers was a beauty of an ethereal sort. She was fair and slightly built, a bit taller than average. Her hair gleamed as pale as moonshine in the flickering stage lights, and her eyes did not need the makeup smudged around them to make them appear large, wide set, and very, very blue.

It was obvious that she was nervous because of the boisterous crowd—it was her first performance—but even so, she moved with natural grace and her voice, though tending to tremble now and then, carried clearly to the gallery where every speech was met with a noisy appreciation that bogged down the limping drama almost to a standstill. And when Emilia declared that wives had as much right to be unfaithful to their spouses as husbands did, it really seemed that there'd be no going on. Looking virginal, angelic, and totally miscast, she declaimed " '. . . and have not we affections, Desires for sport, and frailty, as men have?' " The drunken audience rose lustily to its feet in a noisy clamor of volunteers to help prove the truth of Shakespeare's thesis.

Except for one. The young actress had noticed the dark-haired man in the stage-box seat before. His evening black-and-white had stood out starkly against the background of military red, as had the fact that he was a gentleman. But now his demeanor provided an even greater contrast to the rest of the audience than that supplied by clothes or breeding. While all around the theater men rose noisily to their feet to stamp, cheer, and whistle, he alone stayed seated, his taut face expressionless. "But he should learn to close his eyes if he wants to hide his feelings," Louisa decided privately with an actress's need to file away emotions for future use, even as she smiled and bowed. "His stare gives him away."

For if eyes could be said to sneer, his did so. "He's a critic, I suppose." Louisa almost giggled at the thought, but another stolen glance at the hostile gentleman cost her all desire to laugh. Indeed, she barely restrained a shiver under his icy gaze. Was there something vaguely familiar about the man? She searched her memory to match some former acquaintance with this hard-featured, nearly handsome face. He must be a stranger, she decided. Once met, he'd not easily be forgotten. She was sure of that. "I wish he'd throw something like everybody else and get whatever it is that's angered him out of his system," she decided. "I'd prefer a rotten orange to being glared at."

Then, with an affort, Louisa pushed the hostile critic from her mind and wrenched her attention back to the stage, where Desdemona was also glaring at her. And while the audience kept up its noisy cheering for the minor role, the disgruntled star stalked prematurely from the stage.

The play almost ended at that moment. It took a great deal of persuasion by the director, plus a helpful prick of the lieutenant's sword, to get the leading lady back for her final scene. Back she went, however, and met her pillowed doom to a burst of clapping for her demise, not for her performance. But when the villain Iago ran Emilia through, the audience had had enough and tramped noisily from the theater. The harassed manager signaled to the stagehands, and Othello found himself explaining to the backside of the curtain that he "lov'd not wisely, but too well."

Now the pandemonium behind the stage matched the previous uproar in the pit. The more burly members of the cast and crew stationed themselves at the alley entrance, where a host of suitors were clamoring for a sight of Mrs. Varley, the young Emilia. The defenders' task proved easier than they might have hoped, considering that they were dealing with military gentlemen in fighting trim. But whereas inebriation increased the soldiers' bluster, it also took the edge off their attack. "Gawd 'elp us if this lot's all that stands betwixt us and Bonaparte," one stagehand groaned as he successfully shoved half a dozen grenadiers out the door and bolted it behind them.

The scene now enacted behind the curtain was far more dramatic than the one they'd played when it was raised. Desdemona let out a shriek and hurled herself at the lovely young Emilia. "Upstage me, will you, you bloody whey-faced bitch!" she screeched, and grabbed for Mrs. Varley's long blond locks. She was barely prevented from "snatching the little slut bald-headed" by the agility of her intended victim and a burly stagehand. "Back up, cow, if you don't want your tits sliced off," the young man growled while other stagehands, fresh from their triumph over the military drunks, ran to drag the cursing Desdemona back to her dressing room.

The lieutenant turned his attention to the second lead. "Are you all right, Louisa?"

"Perfectly." Indeed, the young woman seemed remarkably calm, considering the narrow escape she'd had.

The same could not be said of her rescuer. He was clearly agitated, and all the dignity conveyed by his officer's uniform could not conceal his extreme youth. He had tried to rectify that fault and add to his ferocity by raising a military mustache, but the scraggly blond result only emphasized his tender years. There was nothing immature, though, about his anger or in his determination to do something about its cause.

"Get your things, Louisa. Your acting days are over. I'm taking you out of here for good."

"Now just one minute, sir!" The company manager, also player of small parts and stagehand, stopped sweeping splattered fruit to launch a protest. Mr. Scopes knew a good thing when he saw it. He dreamed of his company being hauled from obscurity by the lovely newcomer who had caused such a stir that night. "Mrs. Varley and me have got a verbal contract. I took an awful chance to engage her as she had had no experience whatsoever. And taught her all she knows. And now, just when it looks like she's going to be successful, you tell her to walk out on me! Now I ask you, is that fair?" The short, paunchy middle-aged man glared at the lieutenant as indignantly as he could, given a congenital affliction that kept him blinking rapidly.

"Don't worry, Mr. Scopes," Louisa said soothingly. "Lieutenant Grayson is just upset. I've no intention of walking out. As I told you when I applied, I have nowhere else to go. But tell me"—she looked quizzically at the little man who was mopping his sweaty brow—"was I any good?"

"Good, you ask! Well, I should say so," the manager began heartily. But there was something in the clear intensity of the young actress's gaze that made him fall back on the truth. "Well, as a matter of fact, you've got a far piece to go before you're good. But you could be heard all the way to the gallery, and the way you looked fair took their breath away. I only wish the same could have been said of others," he added darkly. "But besides that—and most important—you've got a sort of quality—a presence—that all the really good ones have. It's something extra there, besides your looks—which are an asset, no mistake—but it's a sort of 'presence,' like I said, that makes an audience sit up and notice you. Like Mrs. Siddons and Mr. Garrick, all the great ones. It's a kind of gift a person's born with, to my way of thinking. Something that can't be learned along with learning stage techniques. Wait and see. You'll be somebody in the theater, m'dear. Mark my words. At least you will be if you don't listen to the likes of him." He blinked rapidly at Lieutenant Grayson, then seemingly assured of the return of his ingenue, he rushed off to try and placate his enraged leading lady.

Lieutenant Adrian Grayson did not seem at all impressed by the manager's rosy forecast of her future on the stage, Louisa noted. But he bit back the rebuttal on his tongue and contented himself with striding back and forth impatiently, getting into the stagehands' way while she removed her makeup and changed her clothes. Then, when the screech of Desdemona drifted out of the star's private dressing room, he stationed himself by the open door of the one shared by the other players. In

7

a remarkably short time, Louisa Varley joined him at the door, looking lovelier than ever in an empire rash-tears satin evening gown, fitted just underneath the bust, then freed to flow long and gracefully down to the ankles. Lieutenant Grayson gaped his appreciation. "I hated all those drunken clods staring at you," he said.

Louisa suddenly recalled an entirely sober stare. But the stage-box gentleman's look of cold dislike was not the sort of thing Adrian referred to. "You mean ogling me the way you are now?" She smiled and took his arm as they left the theater. "Really, Adrian, *I'm* the one hoping to learn the art of acting, and *you're* already performing a Cheltenham tragedy well beyond my level of ability. Come, now. You should be happy for me. After all, I've proven something. I can earn my living on the stage. Mr. Scopes just said so. My future is assured."

The lieutenant was too occupied with trying to round up a carriage to reply just then. But when he'd finally succeeded and had given the direction to the coachman and they were safely ensconced inside, he took up the conversation where he'd left it off.

"There are better ways of assuring your future than by making a spectacle of yourself and being gaped at by every yokel who can scrape up the price of admission to ogle you. For the thousandth time, Louisa, marry me. I'll take care of you."

She laughed softly, reached over, and took his hand. "Please, Adrian, don't be absurd."

"Absurd!" He colored hotly. "Damn it all, Louisa, I love you. Just because I'm a bit younger than you."

"Three years isn't such a 'bit,' but I really wasn't thinking about your age."

"I should hope not. For what that has to say to

anything, I can't imagine. I'm offering to take care of you. I know a lieutenant's pay isn't all that grand, but I'm sure my brother Richard—he's Lord Lyston, I think I told you—will make me an allowance when I tell him I've a wife to support."

Louisa did not actually speak up then and say that Adrian's optimistic assumption hardly tallied with reports she had heard of Richard Grayson, sixth Baron Lyston. Indeed, his lordship was reported to be quite the opposite of his brother, proud to an excess and a veritable high stickler, especially in all matters related to his family. He was hardly the type to welcome an actress for a sister, let alone one with a questionable reputation as well. But, though she kept her silence, there was something in Louisa Varley's attitude that made her companion hasten to refute her unspoken thoughts.

"You don't know Richard at all if you think he's the usual clutch-fisted elder brother. He's the most generous of fellows. He let me wheedle him into buying me a commission, didn't he, and believe me, getting an allowance will be child's play compared to that. For he didn't want me in the army above half."

"No doubt you're right, or you would be under other circumstances," Louisa answered diplomatically. "But in this case, his generosity won't be put to the test. For the thousandth time, Adrian," she said lightly, to take some of the sting out of her words, "I cannot marry you. I am already married."

"That is just what you are not," the lieutenant replied bitterly. "And, my God, Louisa, why can you not simply accept that fact?"

"Because accepting it would make me in my own mind just what I must seem to others—a common whore."

"Louisa, stop it!" The young man seemed alarmed

at a hint of hysteria in her voice. "Don't make me shake you. And don't ever use that word about yourself again."

"Very well, then, I won't. But what about 'fool,' then? You certainly can't deny that it applies."

"I *can* deny it," Lieutenant Grayson retorted stoutly. "What were you when Varley came along—seventeen? Eighteen? Barely out of leading strings. My God, if that villain was able to wheedle Colonel Patrick and the other officers into thinking he was a gentleman, what chance did a green 'un like you have? Lord, you could have knocked the whole regiment over with a feather when it came out that he had a wife and child tucked away in Ireland. Of course, by then a lot of the chaps—me included—had become a bit fed up with him. I mean to say, a lot of things he did and said weren't good *ton* exactly, if you know what I mean."

"I do indeed."

"But even if Varley did come across more like a cit than a gentleman after a bit, when you looked underneath all that surface charm, no one ever suspected that he'd have such a shady background. So I don't know how you could have been expected to tumble to it. Besides," he added regretfully, "he's really a very handsome chap, of course."

"I thought so once," Louisa answered quietly. "But I have not thought so now for a long, long time. Even before his w-wife"—she stumbled over the word a bit—"managed to locate him."

Both lost in thought, they rode in silence for a bit through the crowded streets. Although it was past eleven, the city was still astir and filled with feverish excitement. And as long as the occupants of the carriage kept their eyes upon the crowds and failed to raise them to the foreign architecture, they might have thought, from the uniforms and voices, that they were on their way to a ball in London, not in Brussels.

"Of course I am not the only woman to have been deceived so," Louisa mused aloud.

Lieutenant Grayson longed to change the subject but didn't quite know how to. "No, I guess you aren't," he replied uncomfortably.

"Oh, no, indeed. In fact, perhaps we should form a society, with Mrs. Fitzherbert as our head."

Some thirty years before, Mrs. Fitzherbert had gone through a marriage ceremony with the Prince of Wales and had lived as his wife for quite some time before the heir apparent to the British throne had made his state marriage to Caroline of Brunswick. The debate still raged. Was Mrs. Fitzherbert the Regent's mistress or his wife? But it was not one that the lieutenant cared to get into.

"Of course, Mrs. Fitzherbert had more excuse for her folly than I had," Louisa continued, still talking to herself as much as to Adrian. "After all, she was dealing with the future King of England, whereas I was bedazzled by a gazetted fortune hunter. Poor Nicholas!" She laughed bitterly. "He certainly has been star-crossed. He was so sure that Papa would welcome us back with open arms from Gretna Green. Instead, Papa had all my clothes packed up and waiting. Refused to see me. Had the butler show us both the door."

"The unnatural old—" The lieutenant recalled his company and bit back whatever he had planned to call Lord Faircot.

"At the time I certainly thought he was all you were about to say and more. Now I am not so sure. He had Nicholas spotted for what he was and told me right out what he'd do if I married him. I told Nicholas I'd be disinherited, but he wouldn't believe it. He was sure I could bring my father around eventually. Do you know, till the day he left he never gave up hope that I'd inherit a fortune one day. He certainly underestimated my father's stubbornness. Poor Nicholas." Her lip curled in a sneer. "He had no luck at all. Even after he'd changed his name, his real wife still found him."

"You're the one who's never had any luck, Louisa," Adrian said huskily, reaching over and taking her hand in his. "But I'm going to change all that for you. I want to take care of you, Louisa. I want you to have the protection of my name. And don't start talking rubbish again about already being married. Because you aren't and never have been."

"But that's exactly the point, my dear," she answered gently. "You're right. I'm not married. I never have been. Which means I lived in sin for the past six years with a man who was not my husband. And do you really think I'd drag you down into the mire of scandal with me? Oh no, Adrian. Thank you very much, but I'm far too fond of you for that."

"Mire of scandal? Fustian! The whole world knows that you're an innocent. You married Varley in good faith. No one thinks the worse of you because he turned out to be a villain."

"Oh, do they not?" Her voice was bitter. "Do you know why I finally agreed to go to this ball with you, against my better judgment?"

"Of course I know. I kept badgering you till you said yes."

"That's not the reason. I said yes to give you an object lesson. To let you see firsthand what a social outcast I've become."

"I don't believe it."

"Wait and see. You'll soon find out that I've been tarred with Varley's brush and am now a pariah. And what's more, I'm afraid you'd find that even his lordship, your elder brother, would take as dim a view as the rest of society if his beloved ward should fall into the clutches of an adventuress like myself—a 'fallen woman,' and now an actress to boot. What could be more shocking?"

"You won't be an actress." Lieutenant Grayson set his young jaw stubbornly. "This was your last performance. And Richard needn't hear of it."

"That's where you're wrong, Adrian." Louisa turned toward him on the carriage seat, and by the light of the flickering lamp post, he saw her suddenly smile radiantly. "That's where you're entirely wrong. Do you know that tonight I made a discovery? For the first time in years—since I met Nicholas Varley, in fact—something went right for me. For I found I liked it."

"Liked what?" There was bewilderment in Adrian's voice.

"The stage, that's what. Even in that horrible, smelly theater filled with those poor drunken soldiers and even with that awful barrel of a woman"—she giggled irreverently—"emoting like a fishwife while dodging oranges, I liked it. For there were a few moments there—oh, I know I was awful, as Mr. Scopes admitted—but there were times when for just a second I could feel what it would be like to do it right—to hold an audience in the palm of your hand, to make them laugh and cry and all the rest, just when you wanted to. The power of it! Adrian, just think! And that's what I want to do. It's what I'm going to do. I'll be an actress."

Chapter Two

FOR DAYS THE BALL BEING GIVEN BY THE DUCHESS OF Richmond had occupied the thoughts and conversations of English expatriates in Brussels far more than had Napoleon's inexorable advance. There had been a great scramble to get tickets, but many officers and their wives were doomed to disappointment. War might indeed make strange bedfellows, and some strictures of London society might be set aside on foreign soil. Still, the duchess had her standards.

And Brussels was overflowing with English citizens. It was the headquarters for Wellington's Anglo-Dutch army and teemed with English officers who had been joined there by their ladies to lighten the waiting time until the Corsican made his move. The excuse of these military families for crowding into the city on the eve of battle was that they were necessary to the aid and comfort of their heroes. Others of their countrymen did not find a

14

reason necessary. During the one hundred days of Napoleon's return, the fashionable had come to the Continent in droves, propelled by the same spirit that caused them to attend an opening night or flock to the races. They simply had to be in on everything.

Therefore the Duchess of Richmond had been able to pick and choose as she drew up her guest list. And many were doomed to disappointment as their ordinary backgrounds or lack of social skills kept them off it. But there had been no question concerning Lieutenant Grayson. Not only was he Baron Lyston's brother, but his good-natured friendliness and unconscious air of consequence also made him a favorite. He had been high on the invitation list.

Afterward much would be written and said about the ball, with most accounts exaggerated. But as Lieutenant Grayson and his guest weaved their way through the crush of gold-braided officers and their bediamonded ladies, it would have been difficult for Louisa to doubt any of the extravagances of the claims.

There was a frenzied gaiety in the air that Lord Byron's lines would later define and make immortal.

On with the dance! Let joy be unconfined,
No sleep till morn, when Youth and Pleasure meet,
To chase the glowing Hours with flying feet—

It was as if those dancing there possessed some foreknowledge that, for far too many, Youth and Pleasure were tragically short-lived and must be savored fully before the hours of dawn.

The party was at its height. The Duke of Wellington had just arrived. Louisa and Adrian spied him

15

leaning against a rose-trellis-papered wall holding an animated conversation with his hostess.

"He certainly seems carefree," Louisa whispered. So much for the rumors that the French were on the march. Indeed, the duke might have been smiling and chatting at Almack's Assembly Rooms in London instead of being there in Brussels in the pathway of the enemy's advance.

"Oh, there you are, Grayson, finally!" a voice whooped in their ears. "I've been looking everywhere for you. I've instructions from the duchess to bring you to her the moment you arrive." They turned to see one of Adrian's fellow officers standing behind them, a champagne glass waving in his hand. "Come on, now, there's a good fellow."

Adrian, who had been about to lead Louisa into the quadrille, sighed instead. "Let's go," he said to her. "Let's do the polite first, and then we'll dance."

The young messenger's face reddened suddenly to out-glare the brilliant coat he wore. "Oh, I say. I don't think—" he stammered. "I mean to say—the duchess asked for you in particular. Has a message for you, or some such thing. If Mrs.—er, Miss—would excuse us."

"It's all right, Adrian," Louisa said hastily as her escort's face began to look like a storm ready to break. "Do go on with the lieutenant. It will give me a moment to catch my breath." And, before Adrian could protest, she sat down upon a bench and began to fan herself vigorously.

And indeed, she suddenly was quite uncomfortable—more from embarrassment at her equivocal situation than from the stuffy, crowded ballroom on a summer's night.

Well, she had warned Adrian what her reception would be like. And she had thought that she herself was quite prepared for it. But all the same, she flushed with anger when she saw the colonel's wife from her "husband's" regiment quickly change her course and look in the opposite direction to avoid meeting her. Louisa spotted several other regimental acquaintances there in the ballroom, but no one spoke. She told herself it didn't matter, but nevertheless she was still unable to blot out the hurt. Until her husband was cashiered for bigamy, she had been a favorite. Now her presence at this gathering was clearly an embarrassment for those she'd once considered to be her friends.

A little knot of matrons was sitting out the dance. Louisa's ears were sharp enough to pick up snatches of the whispered conversation. ". . . no better than she ought to be, if you ask my opinion, for all her fine-lady airs. . . . You'll never convince me she didn't know what was what when she ran off with Varley. They say that he . . ."

Louisa had had enough. She turned in the direction of the gossip-mongers and leveled them with a stare, then had the satisfaction of seeing the latest speaker, a captain's wife with whom she'd taken tea a score of times, falter and turn scarlet. Louisa held her head quite high and continued to stare haughtily till the group dissolved in some confusion. Well, if she planned to be an actress, she had to learn to play her parts. And she would die before she would let them see that their spitefulness could hurt her.

Louisa turned back around to face the same direction Adrian had taken. Again, she felt herself under observation. Refusing to use her fan any longer as camouflage, she laid it on her lap and raised her head to meet the next disapproving stare. She hastily snatched the ivory accessory up again, however, and plied it vigorously as she spied the man from the stage-box seat striding toward her.

As his image flickered in and out of sight, she perceived that he was fairly tall and rather younger than she'd supposed there in the theater—in his early thirties, at the very most. Interrupted glimpses revealed the superb cut of his black evening coat across wide shoulders that obviously owed nothing to a tailor's trick of padding. Her peeping did not overlook his ivory satin knee smalls and white silk hose that revealed the muscles of well-shaped thighs and calves. The profusion of snowy lace at his throat and wrists might have appeared foppish on someone else among the high-collared military coats that dominated the ballroom. But it was obvious to Louisa that the gentleman approaching would remain serenely unconscious of any spurious doubts about his manhood.

She hoped against hope that he might pass her by. But all uncertainty was soon erased. She was indeed the target of the man's approach. He came to a halt before her bench and looked her up and down in silence for a moment, as if seeking to reconcile her present image with the character he'd watched so intently on the stage. Louisa lay down her fan and returned his gaze. When it seemed he'd memorized her every feature, the stranger finally spoke. "I'm Lyston."

"Of course," Louisa murmured in reply. "You would be."

She should have known it, there in the opera house. His eyes had been familiar. Their deep blue depths were identical to Adrian's in coloration, but so foreign in expression to his warm and forthright gaze as to have obscured completely that one clue to kinship. And, indeed, all family resemblance between the brothers stopped with the blueness of their eyes.

"I wish to speak privately with you."

Louisa took a moment before replying. Even if she had not seen Lord Lyston in the theater and observed his hostility toward her there, she would still have recognized his appearance here as a confrontation. He was looking down at her now with insolent contempt. And she knew it would take the utmost resolution on her part not to be intimidated.

"I'm sorry," she answered coolly, "but I fear that will be impossible. I am waiting for your brother. I expect him momentarily."

"You needn't. I've arranged with our hostess to keep him occupied. The duchess has promised me twenty minutes. Let's not waste them."

"Really, Lord Lyston, I cannot think we have anything to say to one another. I hardly see why you have gone to so much trouble."

"Oh, do you not? Don't take up my time with games," he snapped. "I've come to Brussels specifically to see you. I can either speak my piece right here, where anyone curious enough to listen can, or we can go to the private apartment the duchess indicated. Which shall it be?"

Louisa shrugged. "Since you seem determined to ignore the fact that I've no wish to speak to you at all, you leave me little choice." She stood. "Lead on, then."

To her dismay, he pulled her into his arms. "Don't worry. I'm not about to make public love to you," he mocked her indignant glare. "Though why an actress should object to that is beyond understanding. Is it not your stock in trade? But never mind. Since we can hardly trudge across the ballroom floor without exciting comment, it seems most sensible to dance across."

The band had begun a waltz, the new craze that was sweeping the Continent but which was still considered shocking back in England. This attitude had always struck Louisa as patently gothic and absurd—until she waltzed with Lyston. As his lordship swept her out upon the floor, his gloved hand seemed actually to sear her waist, and the direction of his gaze and the expression of his eyes made her embarrassingly self-conscious of her décolletage, even though the cut of her gown was quite demure when compared to the majority in the ballroom. Then, when he pulled her far too close even for Continental propriety, and she could feel the sensuous rhythm of his body flowing into hers, Louisa struggled to maintain her composure and a proper distance. "This is not the Cyprian Ball, sir," she said between clenched teeth.

"You're right of course. How strange that I should forget while dancing with a light-skirt," he mocked, then held her fast as she tried to free herself and leave him. He did, however, increase the distance between them just a bit. At the same time he began to circle the ballroom floor once more.

"I thought your time was precious. You were so eager to have a talk."

"It can wait."

He danced with the lithe, easy grace of the natural athlete, and he seemed bent upon sweeping Louisa literally off her feet. It became a point of honor on her part to match him step for step. As they whirled around the ballroom in a rapid, dizzying arc, other less skillful dancers made way for them and stared until finally the music deposited them, flushed and breathless—in Louisa's case, at least—in front of the exit Lyston seemed momentarily to have forgotten.

"Are you all right?" he mocked.

"Of course." To her disgust, her breathlessness undermined her hauteur. "Though I will say I hope I never have to join you on a fox hunt if you make such an athletic event of a mere ballroom dance."

"Don't worry. You are not likely to," he answered, opening the door then escorting her up a flight of stairs and into a small salon. "Which brings me to what I've come to say. Would you care to sit down first?" He gestured toward a Sheraton gilt armchair while he himself walked over to the marble mantelpiece and lit a cheroot from one of the candles placed upon it. He then leaned against the fireplace and "blew a cloud" without so much as a by-your-leave to her, Louisa noted.

"I think I'll stand," she said. "You've surely used up most of the duchess's allotted twenty minutes."

"Then I'll get straight to the point. As I said, I've come to Belgium in order that we might have this little chat. I left London right after I'd been honored—" his lip curled at the word—"by a visit from your lover."

"My what?" Louisa stared at him.

"Your ex-lover then, to be more accurate. Nicholas Varley—in case there have been enough of them to cause confusion." He exhaled a screen of smoke in her direction.

"Nicholas Varley was my husband," she replied with dignity. "Or so I had believed."

"Don't bother to try out any of your wheedles where I'm concerned." Lyston spoke impatiently. "Save that sort of thing for my little brother. I cut my own eyeteeth some years ago. Varley assured me you were well aware of his wife and child when you ran off to the Continent with him."

"And you, of course, believed him."

"Of course."

"And rewarded him for coming to you?"

"Handsomely. I was more than willing to empty my pockets for any information that could save my brother from a scheming actress. A fact Varley was well aware of, naturally."

"Naturally. I never thought he acted from the goodness of his heart. I am a bit surprised, however, that such a 'knowing one,' as you claim to be, could be so trusting. Not everyone relies so on Varley's word."

Lyston shrugged. "His total credibility doesn't concern me. Adrian's infatuation has proven to be an established fact, and Adrian is my responsibility. So what is it worth to you, Mrs. Varley"—the inflection he gave the name turned it into an insult—"to let my little brother off your hook?"

"I fail to understand," Louisa began icily.

"The devil you do not!" he interrupted. "Varley told me that Adrian is so besotted that he has offered marriage. It seems that my brother collared Varley right after he was cashiered and would have tried to thrash the villain if they hadn't been separated. Anyhow, that's when Adrian informed your lover of his 'honorable intentions.' My God, what a *beau chevalier*!" He ground out his cheroot viciously in the fireplace. "Not even to consider offering a *carte blanche*—that is, if he had to get himself entangled with your sort at all. Though I must admit"—he straightened up to face her—"now that I've seen you for myself, I can understand his attitude a bit better than before."

"Thank you."

He ignored Louisa's sarcasm. "All that's beside the point, though. We're wasting too much time. I've urgent business back in London. There's a carriage waiting now to take me to Ghent tonight."

"Oh, dear. You'll miss Napoleon. What a pity," Louisa sneered softly.

"It is, rather." His lordship also chose to ignore her insinuations of cowardice. "Now, then. Let's come to terms. First, has Adrian told you just how his affairs stand?"

"Lord Lyston, this conversation should never even have begun, and I've no intention of prolonging it." Louisa turned to leave the room, but was prevented from doing so by an iron grip upon her wrist.

"Damn it, you will hear me out. Now, get this straight, actress. Adrian has no fortune of his own, nor any prospects other than whatever I choose to settle on him for his lifetime, which will be generous enough—providing he doesn't make a cake of himself by a disastrous marriage."

"In other words, if he lets himself be guided in all things by you," she said between clenched teeth, wincing from the pain.

"Exactly. So if you do marry him, be prepared to live on his military pay, which he alone has never managed to subsist on, I might add. I now make him an allowance."

"Which you would, of course, stop immediately."

"How well you understand. But now I'm prepared to offer you a thousand pounds to turn down Adrian's proposal."

"How handsome of you."

"I consider it to be. Especially now that I've seen you and realize he'll be small loss. You should have his successor lined up in no time." He dropped her wrist, reached into the recesses of his coat, and pulled out a sheaf of banknotes. "I think you'll agree that this is fair." He peeled off some bills underneath her nose. "One quarter on account and the balance to be received when I've heard from Adrian that you've quite blighted his life by rejecting him."

Louisa took the proffered bills and looked at them with interest. "So much? I thought thirty pieces of silver was the going rate."

"A poor parallel, I think. With all his admitted good qualities, Adrian's no Christ—despite a predilection for Magdalens," he added nastily. "But then, I suppose your real intent was to compare me with Judas. That won't wash either, Mrs. Varley. 'St. George' seems a little high-flown perhaps, but it comes closer to the mark."

"With me cast as the dragon?"

"Precisely. I'm more and more impressed with your perceptions. I am quite certain that Adrian would come to thank me in time if he ever realized I was instrumental in his salvation. But did I mention that your silence on that subject is a second condition of your receiving final payment?"

"You did not, but it comes as no surprise. Now, I think, you really must excuse me."

Slowly, deliberately, one by one, she dropped the bills so that they came to rest by the toes of his gleaming pumps. Then she dusted her white gloves together as if to rid them of contamination. "Good evening, Lord Lyston. May I wish you a pleasant— and speedy—trip back home?" Louisa turned her back on him and started for the door.

"Not quite so fast," he growled. "Just what do you intend?"

"Doing about Adrian, you mean?" She turned slowly to face him. "Why, nothing, really. You see, Lord Lyston, you've wasted your time entirely. I've never had the slightest intention of marrying your brother. Though I must admit that now you tempt me. But still, I think not. You see, I'm much too fond of Adrian to risk hurting him even for the considerable satisfaction of scoring over you."

Louisa did not give him time to answer. With

head held high, she made an exit worthy of a larger audience. As she closed the door behind her, she surprised the look of sheer astonishment which had displaced the usual cynicism upon Lyston's face. That glimpse of his discomposure served momentarily as a soothing salve, the only balm available for her injured pride.

Chapter Three

LOUISA SKIRTED THE DANCERS BACK TO THE BENCH where Adrian had deposited her. It was a full five minutes before he came. The duchess, it seemed, had exceeded her commission. Adrian looked annoyed and apologetic.

"I've never seen such a prosy woman," he exclaimed. "I've been trying to get loose for donkey's years, but she rattled on and on. And can you believe it? I've just missed Richard! Of all the beastly luck. The duchess said he was sent over as a courier, or some such thing. At any rate, after he'd seen Wellington, he had to hare it back to London. Blast it all! Richard came here hoping to see me, the duchess said. If I hadn't been at that curst theater—" He stopped abruptly, realizing he was hardly being tactful. "Where's Freddie?" he asked, changing the subject.

"I haven't the slightest idea," Louisa answered. "I haven't seen him since he came to fetch you."

"But I sent him back here with orders to dance with you." He stopped and reddened.

Louisa's laugh surprised even her with its genuineness. "Well, now, being disgraced does have its brighter side when even Freddie Cox is afraid to be seen dancing with me. When I think of all the toes he's trod on, I could almost be grateful to Varley for landing me in this coil.

"But come on Adrian," she went on. "You stand up with me. Your credit can survive it. And who knows when either of us will get another opportunity." She smiled up at him and tossed her head defiantly.

"You're right, damn it." He grinned back. "This is a party, not a wake. First we'll dance, and then we'll have champagne, and then we'll dance again."

"Oh, don't forget the food." She laughed. "I was too scared to eat before the opening. You'd best include the duchess's buffet early on your program."

So dance they did. And as Adrian took Louisa in his arms for her second waltz that evening, she spied Lord Lyston near the exit. Some private demon caused her to nestle closer to her partner and flash a dazzling, triumphant smile toward his lordship. She was rewarded by a murderous look. There was barely time to blow a mocking kiss before her partner spun her in the opposite direction. When she looked for him in the crowd a moment later, it appeared that this time Lord Lyston had truly gone.

Suddenly Louisa did not lack for partners. Perhaps because the gentlemen were more generous than the ladies, perhaps because she'd been seen waltzing with Baron Lyston, or perhaps because she was the most beautiful woman in the room. The lieutenant, however, danced with no one else and, after a bit, refused to share his partner. In fact, he pulled her from a fellow officer's arms as a new set was forming.

"What poor timing, Adrian," Louisa exclaimed, laughing. "You've ruined my little triumph. I quite longed to dance with Charlotte Matthew's husband. She's been pulling my character to shreds all evening."

"It ain't at all funny." Adrian frowned. "I can't bear to see you treated like dirt by people your own father wouldn't allow in his withdrawing room."

But suddenly his lady wasn't listening. As the movements of the dance permitted, she'd been staring at an agitated group gathered around the Duke of Wellington.

"Adrian, something's happened. I think a messenger has just come in."

Wellington, who a moment before had been laughing and joking with those around him, now looked very grave.

"Hadn't you better see what's happening?" Louisa felt more and more alarmed as she saw some of the officers leave the ball hurriedly.

"No." Adrian pulled her close. "There will be time enough for that."

But when the music had finished, he did leave to join the whispering group gathered around the Duke of Wellington.

In a moment, Adrian returned. "Well, this is it." He smiled ruefully. "The courier says that Napoleon's crossed the Sambre and has captured Charleroi. Blücher's Prussians have taken to their heels, and we're going to their rescue in the morning."

"Oh, dear God," she whispered. "We must get you home."

"Why? We can't march till first light. And I'm not going to squander precious time that I can spend with you."

"But you must rest and get your kit together—do a thousand things."

"Louisa," he said sternly, "pull yourself together. If you're going to be a soldier's wife, you have to learn to accept this sort of thing."

She opened her mouth to remind him she had been a soldier's wife for six long years, but then closed it quickly. He was much too dear to risk upsetting him at such a moment.

For Adrian had been the one person in her husband's regiment with whom she'd felt real kinship. He alone came from the same sort of background she'd taken so for granted until Nicholas Varley had come along to part her from that life forever.

Louisa had never mentioned her past, except to Adrian. Indeed, she'd forbidden Nicholas to ever speak of it. But he had, of course. Constantly. Except to Lord Lyston, where the truth about her background could have weakened her scandal value.

During their "marriage," Varley had had a great need to let it be known—always in strictest confidence, of course—that his wife was the daughter of Lord Faircot. But Louisa knew that hardly anyone believed him. It had not taken his fellow officers long to know that Varley and the truth rarely drove in tandem. And when their wives had dropped veiled hints to Varley's wife about her noble background and she had looked embarrassed and changed the subject quickly, that was all the evidence they needed to dismiss the story as one more of the Banbury tales for which Varley was becoming famous.

Adrian, however, had been far more perceptive and had finally wormed the truth out of Louisa. The moment Lord Lyston's brother had joined the regiment, the social-climbing Varley had taken the young man under his wing. Adrian had soon spotted Varley for a toad-eater, but by that point he was in love with Varley's wife and continued to show up regularly at their residence. And Louisa gradually grew to value him like a younger brother. If she worried sometimes that the young man was growing too fond of her in quite a different way than she'd intended, she'd shrugged it off as a boyish calf-love. Now she was not so sure. War could change boys into men quite suddenly. In spite of his tender years and the downy mustache, Adrian's youth was at an end, and he would shortly be called upon to play a grown man's part. If what he wanted now was to dance the night away with her, then that was what they'd do.

The musicians were tuning up again, though now more faltering than eager. Many of the guests were leaving, but others, including the Duke of Wellington, remained. As the band struck up another waltz, Louisa allowed herself to be led out onto the floor. Then the somber mood began to change. For somehow the waltz sparked a heightened romantic frenzy to seize the moment and make it last, as young officers held their ladies close and even dared to snatch a kiss when they felt no one was looking. "Louisa, I do love you," Adrian murmured in her ear in one such stolen moment.

She hoped he'd blame her lack of breath for the fact she did not reply.

At the conclusion of the waltz, Louisa took Adrian by the hand and led him toward the supper table. "You must eat something," she told him sternly. "Heaven only knows when you'll get another chance."

The duke and his aides had left by now. But others lingered on in renewed gaiety, as if there were no such thing as a Napoleon or a tomorrow. But

Louisa was determined that Adrian should go home and snatch a bit of sleep before dawn. First she would make sure he ate. She piled a plate high for him from the cold collation. She supervised his every bite and rationed his champagne. She herself had suddenly lost all appetite and succeeded in choking down only a bit of cold chicken and some fruit. Then she led the protesting Adrian out into the street.

Despite the hour, Brussels was wide awake and frantic with activity. Trumpets were sounding in those sections of the city that quartered soldiers, while drums added their tattoos to help call men to arms. Houses glowed from top to bottom with candlelight as the inhabitants made their soldiers ready to march off to war. Many of their comrades were already on the streets scurrying toward the drumbeats with bayoneted rifles in their hands and knapsacks on their backs.

Adrian commandeered a carriage and gave Louisa's direction to the driver. But she quickly countermanded his order and bade the coachman take them first to Adrian's rooms. When they pulled up before the house where he was quartered, he took her in his arms. "Please, Louisa, don't pull away from me," he said huskily. "I know you don't love me yet. But I promise you, you will. I'll make you forget that villain Varley if it's the last thing I ever do."

"Adrian, you mustn't," she protested. "You mustn't get involved with me. Can't you understand that?"

"All I understand is that I love you. And, oh, Louisa"—his voice broke—"I know it's a shabby thing to say, but I don't think I can face what's coming without some assurance that you'll have me when I come back. Please, Louisa, say you'll marry me."

She started to tell him for the hundredth time that it was impossible. For she had meant what she had said to Lyston. But one look at Adrian's drawn, pale face stopped the rejecting words as they were forming on her lips. There'd be a better time for them—after the battle was over, when the world might possibly right itself once more. Adrian saw the conflict on her face and held her tighter. "You will, then, won't you? Say it, Louisa. Say you'll marry me."

In her mind's eye a frowning vision of Lord Lyston shook his head angrily. But Lyston wasn't here. Nor did he have to deal with this new set of circumstances. "If that's what you really want," she said. The words were barely audible, but they were enough for Adrian. He began to kiss her hungrily— her eyelids, her lips, her neck—until she finally mustered enough strength to push him away.

"Adrian," she said sternly, "you must go. Promise me you'll rest awhile." If she realized she was sounding more maternal than loverlike, he took no notice.

"Yes, ma'am." He gave a solemn, soldierly salute.

"And put something to eat in your cloak pocket."

"Yes, ma'am."

"And a flask of brandy."

He kissed her passionately once more. "Who needs brandy after that?" he grinned.

But this time Louisa succeeded in shoving him out the carriage door, and he reluctantly bade the driver take her home.

The coach route took them through the Place Royale that was already thronged with congregating soldiers. Some were taking tender leave of their sweethearts or their wives and children. Some were sitting quite unconcernedly on the pavement waiting for their comrades to arrive. Others even managed to sleep on packs of straw while baggage wagons were being loaded, shouting officers went riding by, carts rumbled upon cobblestones, horses neighed, drums beat, and bagpipes shrilled, all in noisy prelude to the war.

After Louisa reached her own set of rooms that occupied the second story of a doctor's house, she changed her ball gown for a morning dress, brushed out her hair from its Grecian style, and lay down upon her bed. But it was impossible to sleep. First light found her seated by her bedroom window. When the drums began their purposeful, ominous roll, she stepped out upon her small balcony and stood shivering in the early morning air.

The sun was just rising as the parade came down the street below her. And a gallant sight it was, with the band at the head of the column playing the regimental march. The company major rode a fine white charger that seemed actually to strut proudly to the music's cadence. Then came the grenadiers with their captain at their head. In the column's center were the colors, carried by two ensigns, both young enough to break Louisa's heart. Then Adrian appeared, marching bravely at the head of his own men, looking dashing and handsome and jaunty in his scarlet uniform. He glanced up, and his face lighted in a smile as he saw her standing there in her white morning dress with her flaxen hair tumbling down about her shoulders. She smiled and waved, then blew a kiss, fighting hard to hold back the tears till he could no longer see her.

But then she let them flow, and they continued long after the column was out of sight and the trumpets and the drumbeats had died down to a faintly drifting echo. Nor did they slacken when Louisa finally stopped staring at the empty street and turned and went inside.

Chapter Four

*L*OUISA JERKED AWAKE AND SAT UPRIGHT IN ALARM. She stared at the small enameled clock on the mantel, seeking some logical reason for her startled agitation. "Oh my goodness, I am late!"

She had gone back to bed shortly after the army marched out of Brussels, but had lain wide-eyed while the events of the last few hours whirled like a kaleidoscope inside her brain to finally slow down, then halt and focus in upon her theatrical debut. She savored again those fleeting moments when she had almost been Emilia and had felt what it must be like to be an actress. Then she had faced the fact that for most of the performance she had been truly awful, though not so bad as Mrs. Collins, she recalled with a drowsy giggle. Mrs. Collins! She opened one sleepy eye and squinted at the clock again. "She really *will* snatch me bald-headed this time," she said outloud, knowing she should give the leading lady no new excuse for enmity by keeping the rehearsal waiting, but still unable to drag herself from the bed in which she'd slept alone for ages now, even before Varley's legal wife had made her disastrous appearance. Just a wink or two more. I can tell them the storm delayed me, she thought, listening to the distant thunder. She almost succeeded in dozing off again, but was prevented from actually doing so by the memory she'd been trying hard to keep at bay by dwelling on the performance of the night before. Now there was no dodging it. She had promised to marry Adrian Grayson.

She groaned aloud. But what else could I have done? she asked her prodding conscience. The French are Adrian's enemy, not I. I couldn't let him go off to war troubled over me. That would have been too cruel. He'll understand, she thought, hazily drifting off again. Adrian's very understanding. He knows I do care for him, though not in the way he'd like me to. He'll see that I wanted to give him peace of mind. To send a soldier into battle thinking he had no one to live for would be worse than heartless. It could even prove fatal for him, cause him to take unnecessary risks, march into the cannon's mouth ...

"Oh dear God, the cannons!" Louisa sat upright once more, fully awake this time, a look of horror on her face as the significance of the dull pounding sound that had awakened her in the first place now dawned on her. There it was again! Rolling in the distance like the sound of a summer storm, only more regular and persistent in its deadliness.

She leaped to her feet and ran out on her balcony, unconscious of her tousled hair and rumpled dress. The sight that met her eyes increased her panic. All was confusion, with people running in and out of their houses as if undecided whether to flee or barricade themselves inside. Others were flocking to the small church down the street—to pray for their fighting men, most likely, and for their own safety without a doubt. The English families were piling into their carriage prepared for flight.

"What's happening?" Louisa leaned over the balcony and screamed. Lady Patrick, who had come to Brussels with her daughter to join her colonel husband, had stopped speaking to Louisa some weeks before. But this was no time for social niceties.

"He's coming!" she shrieked, shoving her daughter and a valise inside the carriage. "The Corsican Monster's coming! They say he has cut our armies in two and will be here tonight!"

And to the accompaniment of her daughter's shriek to "Hurry!" she jumped inside and her coach clattered down the street.

For a moment, Louisa shared their panic. She wanted to scream for them to wait—there was room in the coach for her, they must not leave her here alone and unprotected. With an effort, though, she got hold of herself and shrugged. *"C'est la vie,"* she murmured philosophically, then grimaced at her unconscious lapse into the language of the enemy. Nothing like being prepared for the worst, she thought.

Louisa stoically pushed from her mind all she'd heard of French atrocities. They say the same of our men, she thought, but the idea offered little comfort. "If they come, perhaps I can pass for Belgian. I speak French like a native, or nearly so," she assured herself, pausing before the glass to tidy her hair. But a second glance at her reflection canceled out that hope. Her blue eyes and flaxen hair would no doubt betray her background even if her tongue did not. Oh, well. At least the prospect of invasion should be an acceptable excuse for being late to a rehearsal, she thought wryly as she put on her bonnet, added a light shawl of Norwich silk to hide her rumpled dress, and went out into the street.

Her journey to the theater took her diagonally across a park flanked by several hotels jammed with English guests. Here the pandemonium among her fellow countrymen made Louisa's frenzied street seem almost tranquil by comparison. Some, like Louisa's fortunate neighbor, Lady Patrick, were already packed for flight. But the majority were finding that horses had become more scarce in Brussels than elephants. And those steeds that were available were going to the highest bidder at prices that would have bought an entire stable back in England.

And still the rumors flew. Louisa paused occasionally to clutch at some passerby and ask what the latest news was. The answer was always basically the same. "Napoleon is on the march toward Brussels. The English will never stop him. He'll be here tonight."

Napoleon! The name alone seemed to have the power to strike terror. "He's only a man," Louisa reflected stoutly. "A little man, at that. He was stopped before and forced to abdicate to Elba. He'll be stopped again. The English won't be beaten." But all the same, she shivered.

No echo of the bedlam of the night before remained to haunt the theater. It was, in fact, eerily sepulchral as Louisa opened the stage door and stepped inside. No one else had come, it seemed. She chided herself for being so foolish as to have thought they would. The idea of actually rehearsing three hours of make-believe while the world tumbled about their ears was too absurd! Still, she shrugged, she had to be somewhere, after all, and walking to the theater had been as good a way to pass the time as any. Then a low murmur of voices caught her ear. It seemed that some other actors had been of the same opinion. Louisa walked out on the stage and found half a dozen of the company seated there, saying little but shooting frightened glances at one another.

Mr. Scopes's eyes opened wide in surprise, then blinked rapidly when he saw her. "Ah, well, now, here's our newest family member. Welcome, Mrs. Varley. We thought you'd be halfway to Ostend by now with some of your influential friends."

"I'm afraid not," Louisa answered lightly. "The only influential friends I have are gone in quite the opposite direction—to meet Napoleon."

"Gawd 'elp 'em." Mr. Draper, who played Othello, crossed himself, quite forgetting to be theatrical, sounding almost cockney.

"Take a load off your feet, dearie." Miss Nell Scopes, who was the manager's ancient aunt, the company wardrobe mistress, character actress, and general factotum, spoke up cheerfully and nodded to a chair, which Louisa drew into the huddle on the stage. Miss Nell seemed to share none of the general panic. She was stitching a rip in one of Desdemona's gowns and humming as unconcernedly as if all wars were figments of a playwright's imagination and could be ended with a lowered curtain. She peered over the top of her spectacles at Louisa and gave her a near-toothless grin. "It's an ill wind that blows no good, dearie, and all that sort of flummery. You're now the leading lady of the internationally famous Scopes Theatrical Company, in case you didn't know it." And she cackled delightedly.

"Whatever do you mean?" Louisa asked.

"She means that Mrs. Collins has fled for home," Mr. Draper answered for her. "And thank the Corsican for that much, at least. If I'd of had to drag that old behemoth round the stage much longer, I'd have smothered her for real."

"And since that just leaves two females"—Old Nell's shoulders shook—"Scopes there has picked you for Mrs. Collins's replacement over me. At least he said as how he would if you showed up again, which of course he doubted, but now you have, so there it is. Wonderful how he weighed your face against my experience and you got the post. But there it is. Rank discrimination, I call it. Here you are the company's leading lady after only one performance—and a partial one at that. Lord love us, just wait till Mrs. Siddons gets wind of you, m'dear. If she won't shake in her boots for sure! Why, if you should make it through a second night, you'll probably take over Covent Garden." She chuckled delightedly at her humor, twisting her jaw until it almost dislocated, then managed to line up two remaining teeth and snapped off the thread.

Nell Scopes's cheerfulness relieved some of the tension. The other players relaxed a bit, and there was a great deal of discussion about what the company should do next. This was simply an exercise in time-filling futility since all decisions were out of their hands. Mr. Scopes had already tried in vain to find them transportation back to England, but he had been unable to outbid his wealthy countrymen for Belgian horses.

"What about last night's receipts?" Mr. Draper looked at the manager suspiciously. "The place was packed. That should have brought in a bit of brass."

"Might have done, if your brave fighting men had paid," Aunt Nell answered for her nephew. "But the bulk of 'em showed me their sabers in lieu of tickets." She chuckled. "Said as 'ow it was me 'patriotic duty to let 'em in seein' as 'ow they was off at any time to die for king and country,' " she mimicked.

"Well, wot do we do now?" Jeremiah Scopes, the manager's fifteen-year-old son, asked in a voice that his best efforts couldn't stop from quavering.

"Why, for one thing," his great-aunt said with a chuckle, "you'd best start learning Emilia's lines. Since Mrs. Varley here has been promoted on up to Desdemona and we're fresh out of females, we'll just do as Old Will Shakespeare intended and put a boy in a woman's role."

"I'll be damned before I dress up like some curst female!" Young Scopes's indignation momentarily overcame his fear, which may well have been what his great-aunt had had in mind.

"Do you speak French?" Mr. Draper asked Louisa.

"Yes. Why do you ask?"

"Well, the French are coming, and we're out of money. So if they don't kill us all or worse, and we hope to eat, we'd better play to them."

"I don't think it will come to that." Louisa noted with what must have been professional detachment that she sounded much more confident than she really felt. "Our English soldiers will halt Bonaparte in his tracks. You wait and see."

But shortly afterward, as she hurried back toward home, Louisa recalled the words as sheer bravado. The rest of the company had decided to stay together in the theater and await whatever came, and they had begged her to stay there with them. But she'd pooh-poohed the notion of any personal danger. Wellington would hold the French. They'd see. But now that she was away from the make-believe atmosphere of center stage, she was none too sure.

The city was beginning to fill up with Belgian deserters who had broken and run in face of the French onslaught. They had retreated right through the ranks of the advancing British, a circumstance that could not have done much to bolster English spirits. Now they filled Brussels with blood-chilling accounts of the might of the enemy. The deserters concluded each recitation with a dire prediction of the destruction of the British Army, which was now fighting at Quatre Bras, where the sound of cannon fire could still be heard.

Louisa clutched at passersby and called out to carriages being loaded in the street, hoping against hope that the latest bit of news might be encouraging. None was. "They've taken Wellington a prisoner," one elderly English gentleman shouted back as he whipped the horse he sat upon and bolted toward the coast. "The British Army is in full flight!" a Belgian farmwoman shrieked as she scuttled homeward with her baskets of unsold cabbages.

The panic was contagious, and Louisa started to run toward home. After racing up the stairs, she arrived breathless and panting in her rooms. She locked the door behind her quickly and slid a heavy commode against it, feeling foolish as she did so, as if a piece of furniture could stop the enemy. She stood a moment breathing heavily from fear and exertion. It was only when her blood had ceased its deafening pounding in her ears that Louisa felt an odd sensation of something changed. But it was several seconds longer before she realized just what had made the difference. Silence. An eerie silence. As terrifying suddenly as the dull, relentless pounding had been before. She rushed out upon her balcony and looked toward the south. Nothing could be seen in the rapidly falling darkness except the flickering of candles here and there in those houses where there still were occupants. Louisa strained her ears in an effort to pick up some sound on the light breeze that was blowing in her face. But all was silence. The cannons were quiet at Quatre Bras.

Louisa was awakened at dawn next day by the sound of wagon wheels and rushed again to her balcony to see what was happening. Instead of the enemy she expected, she saw the allied wounded making a heartbreaking trek back into the city. Their pathetic, straggling column seemed a nightmarish travesty of the jaunty parade that had marched off so bravely to the sound of pipes and drums only a few hours before.

Some casualties were loaded into carts on piles of straw, their bayonets sticking out like pitchforks ready to be seized, though it was doubtful if any of the men could now make use of them. Those wounded who had both the means and strength to be on horseback were usually the more fortunate ones. But Louisa shuddered as she saw one mounted officer, his face completely swathed with bandages, being led by his horse's bridle. Most walked, as best they could, with the weaker ones leaning on their stouter comrades for support. Civilians were rushing into the street to give them aid. Many soldiers were being pulled out of the grisly procession and carried into homes.

Louisa leaned over her balcony and was about to call out an offer of a bed when she heard a fearsome hammering on her door. She ran to answer, half-expecting it to be off its hinges when she got there. "Mrs. Varley, are you home?" a deep voice shouted. "For God's sake, open up!"

"Who is it?" she called, looking apprehensively at the commode whose drawers had rattled open from the pounding. "What do you want?"

"It's Private Webster, ma'am. Come from Lieu-tenant Grayson. He's hurt bad. For God's sake, open up!"

Louisa shoved away the commode and dragged back the heavy door bolt. She opened the door a crack and barely checked a scream. The soldier who stood there was a ghastly sight, smeared with blood from his shako to his gaiters. His face at one time might have seemed painted with a bright red brush, but now the surface had turned a dark, dull brown and was in the process of flaking off. The brilliant red of his military coat had been soaked in patches to a darker hue. And there were dark smudged prints on the shiny visor of his cap where he'd reached up with bloody fingers to adjust it.

"Come in," Louisa gasped. "I'll try to fetch a doctor."

"No, you come with me!" The soldier had forgotten all forms of polite address in his agitation. "I ain't the one what's hurt. Leastways not to speak of. Most the blood's from the lieutenant. He's hurt that bad." And suddenly tears appeared in the private's eyes, then coursed a slow and crooked path down his crusted cheeks. Even in her agitation, Louisa was touched that this big, tough-looking soldier should give way to tears. "I don't think he's gonna make it, ma'am," he choked. "And he's asking for you. Seeing you's all that's kept the life in him so far. For God's sake, hurry!"

"Where is he?" she asked as they rushed out into the street. Heads turned to stare at the blood-smeared soldier and the young woman wrapped in a flowing morning robe, her hair still tumbled down upon her shoulders.

"At Lady Follett's rooms in the Hotel du Parc, ma'am. He'd hoped to make it all the way to your place, but the jolting was too much. We'd come partway in the carts, you see. So when we was passing the hotel, I had 'em stop, and I carried him in. The Folletts are neighbors of the Graysons. It was the only thing left to do." The private was obviously not happy with his decision, and Louisa recalled a haughty lady riding in an open carriage through the park who had pretended not to see Adrian's perfunctory bow. He had sworn then underneath his breath and, when Louisa asked, he had reluctantly identified the woman as a "stiff-rumped neighbor from Somerset." Since the lady had refused to acknowledge her upon that occasion, Louisa hardly expected to be received cordially now.

All was chaos in the hotel suite. Boxes were being dragged into the middle of the floor, half-packed. Servants were dashing back and forth cramming things into them, then snatching the articles out again to be replaced with others of greater value. Lady Follett was standing in the midst of the confusion, wringing her hands, screaming conflicting directions to the servants, and talking in agitated, heavily accented French to a Belgian cleric. Her agitation was overridden by tight-lipped disapproval as Louisa and the private burst into the room.

"I do not approve of this, Mrs. Varley—or whatever you now call yourself," she said. "Nor will Lord Lyston. I want that clearly understood. Any ceremony here takes place over my stringent objections. As for you, Webster"—she glared at the soldier with total disregard for his blood-streaked countenance and near exhaustion—"you may be sure I shall render Lord Lyston a full accounting of your part in this disgraceful affair. He will not be pleased. Be assured of that!"

"That's as may be." The private seemed pushed well beyond all class distinction and glared at her ladyship. "But then I don't guess as how his lordship had to listen to a dying lad's pleadings, did he now?

"You there, come on, double-quick!" Webster forestalled Lady Follett's answer by barking at the priest. The cleric did not seem to understand the words but rightly interpreted the urgency of the tone and the direction of the gesture. He moved with Louisa and the soldier toward the bedchamber.

Louisa tugged at Webster's arm. "I don't understand," she whispered. "Is he here for the last rites?" How Lady Follett, Protestant though she no doubt was, could object to such a ceremony was more than she could fathom.

"No," Webster said, pulling her on with him, "he's here to marry you. Now hurry, for God's sake, or we'll be too late."

"Marry!" Louisa gasped. "But that's impossible. I've no intention of—"

The six hours of bloody battle and the struggle of getting his wounded charge back alive to Brussels was taking its toll of Webster. "Look here, ma'am." He glared at Louisa. "I don't give a tinker's damn what you want or don't want to do. All I know is that that there young fellow's had just one thing on his mind ever since a bullet brought him down, and I only got to him after he'd been trampled by the whole goddamned—begging your pardon, ma'am—French cavalry. And that was to see that you were taken care of. It's all that's kept him alive up to now.

"Now I came to this godforsaken place for just one reason—to look after Master Adrian for his lordship. And if you think I'm not going to see to it that the lad's last request is granted, then you just don't know Samuel Webster. And if you're so caperwitted as not to want to be married to about the finest lad I ever knew"—his voice broke again—"well, just never you mind, for that's not going to be much problem for you, ma'am, because I reckon if he lives out the day, it'll be a miracle. Now, come on, will you." And he took her by the arm again and tugged her into a bedchamber behind the priest.

"Is that you, Louisa? It's too dark to see you." The voice was so weak as to be barely audible.

A parlormaid seated by the high four-poster bed rose and backed away respectfully. Louisa sat down in the vacated chair and grasped the cold hand groping toward her. She took full note of the clouded eyes and the sunshine streaming in the windows. "I'm here, Adrian," she said gently as tears welled at the sight of the pale face and the oozing bandage on his shoulder. "Sssh, you mustn't try to talk." She took up the cloth from a basin filled with bright pink water and wiped at the trickle of blood stealing out from the corner of the lieutenant's mouth.

"It was the tramplin' that done for him, ma'am," Private Webster murmured in her ear. "The ball got him in the leg and knocked the pins from under him, and he was bayoneted in the shoulder. Then the horses were on top of him before I could get to him."

"Louisa." Except for the relentless bloody trickle, the lieutenant's face was whiter than the linen of the bed. "I'm done for. But I made Webster promise he'd get us married. And then—afterward—he'll take you back to England. Back to Graylands. To my brother. Richard will look after you. He's good at that sort of thing. Tell her, Webster. He's used to taking care of all of us." His mind seemed to be wandering. He paused and coughed. The blood increased alarmingly.

"Got to hurry," Adrian murmured. "Tell the parson to get on with the ceremony."

"Do it, ma'am," Webster hissed as Louisa hesitated. "Tell that Frog to tie the knot. I mayn't have been able to save the lad, but by God I'll have his lordship know that I saw to it he died easy. Now tell that heathen to get on with it!"

But the priest needed no further telling. Either he understood some English, or the private communicated on quite another level. At any rate, he asked the parlormaid to move closer to act as a witness while he leaned over the dying man and began to recite the vows.

Louisa was dimly aware, possibly from a sudden chill in the atmosphere, that Lady Follett had stepped into the room. The lieutenant's words were barely audible. "I Adrian, take thee, Louisa—"

"Till death do us part." When the abbreviated ceremony was completed, Adrian sighed and closed his eyes. "I love you, Mrs. Grayson," he whispered.

"And I love you," Louisa answered gently, leaning over to kiss his forehead.

Time now seemed suspended. Louisa sat by the bed holding the cold young hand that grew gradually colder despite all her will to warm it. She was barely conscious that the priest had left and that the maid had placed another chair beside hers for Webster. He too sat immobile, his eyes intent on his charge's face. Finally it was he who spoke. "I reckon he's been gone for some time now, ma'am."

Then he reached across and gently unclasped her hand. "There's no more we can do for him now. Except to make sure his body's finally took back to England."

Like two sleepwalkers, they made their way out of the death chamber. "He's gone, ma'am," Webster

48

informed Lady Follett, who was dressed in traveling clothes, ready for departure.

Her ladyship's first reaction was obvious relief that she could flee now with a clear conscience. But "God rest his soul," she murmured piously. "I'll send someone for that priest again. I've already paid him to put the poor lad in his churchyard until this horrible war is over and Lyston can take him home to Graylands. And what Lyston will say to this scandal I don't even want to think. If only he could have stayed in Brussels a little longer, this would have never happened. I shall assure him that I did my best to stop such an unseemly desecration of his brother's last few moments upon this earth.

"And as for you"—she turned to glare haughtily at Louisa—"I shall do my utmost to see that all your scheming comes to nothing. A woman of your reputation taking advantage of a poor boy on his deathbed! Well, it won't do, I warn you. It's not only immoral, it's bound to be illegal, too, as I intend to inform his lordship the moment I set foot on English soil. Married in French indeed! Whoever heard of anything so rackety? Well, you'll never see a shilling of the Grayson fortune, let me assure you. His lordship will spot you for what you are, all right. You might have been able to pull the wool over that poor innocent lad's eyes, but you won't fool Lord Lyston. He's much too knowing to be taken in by a regimental light-skirt."

"Now, see here, ma'am," Webster had begun, but Louisa pushed him before her out into the hall. Lady Follett continued muttering in shocked disapproval while at the same time berating her harried staff to hurry with the packing. The closing door mercifully cut off the unpleasant sound.

"Well, she's right about one part, at any rate,"

Louisa remarked as the two of them trudged wearily toward her home. "There can't have been anything legally binding in such a ceremony."

"I wouldn't be too sure of that, ma'am," the private answered. "The lieutenant got that special license all right and tight some time ago. For he'd hoped to marry you before he had to go off and fight. Nobody expected Boney to call this soon, and that's a fact.

"Now it's true I may have given that Frenchie priest I got the impression that the lieutenant was a Catholic—which he never was. Leastways, that's how I imagine it must of come out in the foreign tongue since the priest was so willing and all and didn't question the bloke what was doing the translating. Of course the brass I gave him to do the thing made him a lot less curious, too. But still it seems to me as how all that's more a church matter than a legal one. So I'd say you're married right and tight. And in Lieutenant Grayson's mind, the marriage was true enough—and begging your pardon, that's all that really counts. For the boy was dead set"—the private winced here at his choice of words—"on you having his name after you'd lost the use of Varley's, so to speak. So if you'll excuse my saying so, I think you owe it to the lad to use it. Seeing it was his dying wish and all. I'm telling you, ma'am, he was that obsessed with seeing that you took his name and putting you under the protection of Lord Lyston, that it kept him alive against all odds till the thing was done. So you can't treat this marriage as anything but true. It would be a betrayal."

Private Webster looked near the breaking point himself. Louisa laid a hand gently on his arm. "Don't worry, Webster. If Adrian wished me to be Mrs. Grayson, that's what I will be. I didn't lie, you know, when I told him that I loved him. It may not have been in the way he wanted, for I won't deceive you. Under normal circumstances, I'd not have wed him. But I did love him. I grew to love him dearly at a time when I'd never thought to care for anyone or anything again." She hadn't realized that she was crying until she watched the tears run down the soldier's face and felt the dampness of her own.

They'd arrived back at Louisa's doorstep, and Webster brushed at his face with the back of a bloody sleeve. "I hope God will forgive me, ma'am, but I'm going to have to break my word to Adrian Grayson now and leave you. I got no choice. I need to get back to my company fast as I can. I feel like a Judas, deceiving a dying man that way, but soon as the battle's over, I promise I'll be back. The thing is, I'd be a traitor and a coward if I didn't go. They're going to need me bad. I didn't reckon as how it made much difference leaving when I did right after we'd stopped things for a bit at Quatre Bras. But that little skirmish was just a warmup for what's coming. It's Boney himself we'll have to contend with now, and they'll need every man jack they can get their hands on to stop him. And I guess by now they'll be wondering what's become of me."

"You mean they don't know where you are?" She stared at him. "You just deserted?"

"No, ma'am. I wouldn't call it that." His face set mulishly. "Like I told you, my first duty was to see to Lieutenant Grayson. That's what I came to this curst country for. But now that's finished, I'm going back to my outfit. I'm no deserter."

"I know you aren't," Louisa said hastily. "You couldn't be. But you aren't going anywhere till you've rested and had some food." Overriding the private's protests, she made him go upstairs with

51

her and sit down a bit while she sliced bread and prepared eggs for him. She even succeeded in unearthing a bottle of brandy that Varley had left behind. Webster took a grateful swig, then, at her insistence, put the bottle in his pocket for future reference.

"What did you mean when you said you'd come to Belgium to look after Adrian?" Louisa asked after the soldier had slaked his appetite with some voracious bites and slowed down to normal eating speed. She had been right when she'd judged him starved. She had no appetite herself, but sat at the table with him, sipping tea.

"Well," the private answered through a large mouthful of crusty bread, "his lordship was dead set against the lieutenant joining up, you see. He'd be ten years older than the boy—the same as me—and he'd been all the father the lad had ever had. The two of us together taught young Adrian to ride and hunt—to do it all, you might say. You see, I worked in the stables there at Graylands. Anyhow, Master Adrian teased his lordship for months. And when it became pretty evident that if his lordship didn't give in and buy his colors for him, the lad would run off and enlist as a regular soldier, which would never have done of course"—the "regular soldier" sounded horrified—"well, then, Lord Lyston broke down finally and bought his commission for him. But then Lord Lyston said as how I'd best go too and look out for the lad." The soldier's hand shook as he put down his tea. "Fair job of work I made of that!" he finished bitterly.

"You can't blame yourself," Louisa protested indignantly. "You couldn't possibly have saved Adrian. Besides, the whole idea was absurd. I can't believe it. You mean Lord Lyston actually ordered you to go into the army? I never heard of anything so feudal!"

"You don't understand, ma'am," the private interrupted stiffly. "It wasn't like you think at all. I wasn't 'ordered' to go. It's just that his lordship and I were always by way of looking after the lad, you see. He'd of come himself, but he had his duties to attend to there, of course."

"Of course," Louisa said sharply. She would have liked to express her opinion of Lord Lyston's odd sense of responsibility further, but she hardly felt it fair to Webster. Nor did she mention his lordship's recent visit, of which the private seemed unaware.

Webster stood. "Now I'd best be getting back."

"But you can't," Louisa protested. "You're exhausted. Rest first. Use my bed. Then you can go."

The soldier wouldn't hear of it however. "I'd best not waste the time. Boney will probably be in a hurry to heat things up again. After all, he doesn't want his bunch to think too long about the licking they just took. Might give 'em some second thoughts. Anyhow, with luck, I'll get some rest. At least I won't have as far to go back as I had getting here," he added philosophically. "The duke's moving back this way."

Louisa insisted that Webster stuff his pockets full of bread and cheese first. Then she walked outside with him.

"I'll be back, ma'am," he told her earnestly. "And I'll see to it you get back to England and to Graylands."

Louisa didn't answer that. It didn't seem appropriate to tell the private that she had no intention of going to Graylands ever. Or that the Great Lord Lyston was the last person in the world she wished to see again. Instead, she said, "Don't worry about me, Webster. I'll be fine. I've theater friends now, you see. I want you to concentrate on taking care of yourself." Then she added, "Oh, Webster, I do want you to know"—she faltered, not quite knowing how to proceed once she'd started—"want you to know that while some of those things Lady Follett said about me were true in one sense—literally true, I'd have to say—" She hesitated once more, not quite understanding why she felt it so necessary to explain herself to this Grayson servant, when she'd never tried to make excuses to her social equals. But somehow she wanted Webster to think well of her for Adrian's sake. "But there were some extenuating circumstances," she continued, "that perhaps wouldn't seem quite so—"

"It's all right, ma'am," the private told her gently. "You don't need to explain a thing to me. You see, I happen to know that Master Adrian wouldn't of married you if you wasn't quality. Master Adrian could never have made that kind of mistake. Goodbye now, Mrs. Grayson. And thank you for everything."

Through a blur of tears, Louisa watched Private Webster stride swiftly off in the direction of Waterloo.

Chapter Five

THE NEXT DAY WAS THE SABBATH. BUT CANNON FIRE not church bells filled the air with sound. From morning till well past sunset, the cannons roared, closer, louder, more terrifying than two days before. Louisa now marveled that the noise of Quatre Bras had frightened her at all.

Then all was silence—followed by dread. Till at last the incredible, the impossible, the glorious news filtered back into the city—the Allies had won the day! Napoleon was halted! This time it would be forever.

Throughout the next few days Louisa often thought of Private Webster and tried to find more acceptable reasons for the fact he'd not returned than the one she kept pushing resolutely from her mind.

Optimism was not difficult these days. If the ultimate in miracles had happened and Napoleon had been stopped—and the near thing it had been was becoming known—then one might pray hopefully for other miracles. So Louisa continued the prayers for Private Webster that had begun with the sounds of Waterloo. But even as she prayed, she prepared for her own immediate departure.

For the victory at Waterloo almost paled in its importance before an event even more astounding. The Scopes Theatrical Company had been offered an engagement to perform in Bath.

Louisa could only chalk up their good fortune to the general euphoria that gripped the city. She crossed her fingers that Mr. Bennett, who owned the hall they'd be playing in, would not change his mind on second thought. Like some long-lost rich relative from an impossible melodrama, he had approached Mr. Scopes on the Monday after Waterloo and had offered the company a booking "on the condition that you fire the fat lady who was Desdemona and make that Mrs. Varley your new lead." For it happened that Mr. Bennett had been among the rowdy spectators at *Othello* who had witnessed Louisa's stage debut. In spite of all the uproar, he had not failed to note the audience reaction to the young newcomer.

First, Mr. Scopes had given Mr. Bennett the good news. Mrs. Varley was already their premier actress. Then, with much embarrassment, he had unburdened himself about their financial crisis. Somehow, without actually lying about the matter, the manager made it appear that one of the thespians who fled Napoleon had also made off with the gate receipts, leaving the company unable to finance the voyage home. This news gave Mr. Bennett momentary pause. He felt he'd already gone far enough out upon a shaky limb just by hiring Scopes's tatty troupe. But finally, in the general spirit of goodwill that all proud Englishmen were feeling at that glorious time, he agreed to finance the actors' journey home.

For Louisa it proved to be a strange feeling to return once more to Bath. The Scopeses and Mrs. Grayson, as she now called herself, journeyed there together on one of the "Flying Coaches" that in the summertime made the run to Bath from London in one day, a speed that Miss Nell Scopes, for one, declared "unnatural." There had been enough daylight left when they climbed stiffly from the coach at York House to make their way on foot to their new location. And it was the direction that they took, even more than the fact that she was probably the first of her family ever to have traveled on a public coach, that drove home to Louisa how greatly her status had changed since her earlier Bath visit.

Before, her route would have led through the Circus to the Royal Crescent, both architectural masterpieces of the father-son John Woods. The Crescent was one of the very few places her father had considered suitable addresses for his ten-year-old daughter and himself. He had been in his mid-fifties then, plagued with inflammation of the joints. His physician had insisted that he take a course of the medicinal waters Bath was noted for.

Even then, in 1802, the city had declined from its former glory. In the mid-eighteenth century, Bath had been second only to London as a gathering place for the *beau monde*, its success having been assured by a succession of royal visits. Then it had been a pleasure resort as much as a health spa, its entertainments and hospitality presided over by a series of masters of ceremonies, the most famous being the great "Beau" Nash, often referred to as the uncrowned King of Bath.

But at the time Lord Faircot had paid his grudging visit, the fashionable had followed the Prince of Wales to the Channel resort of Brighton, and Bath was in the sunset of its fame, more noted as a retirement place for elderly professionals and as a place for invalids of any age to congregate than as the social mecca it once had been.

Still, there was a great deal of amusement to be found—perhaps especially for a ten-year-old—and Louisa recalled nostalgically the hours she had spent patronizing the riding schools, playing on the tennis courts, climbing the hills around the town, stuffing herself with the sweet Bath buns the town was famous for, and visiting Sydney Gardens to watch fireworks, listen to concerts, and run through the labyrinth.

Now it took all her resolution not to be tempted toward self-pity as she turned with Mr. Scopes, his aunt, and son toward an unfashionable section of the town. They trudged slowly, burdened as they were with baggage, while Mr. Scopes squinted at numbers in the deepening dusk until they finally came to a halt before a house in Trim Street.

The pleasure and excitement of her companions as they surveyed their new address nipped in the bud any inclination Louisa might have had to compare this shabby-genteel residence with the palatial beauty of the Crescent. For if her fortunes seemed to be on the wane, the Scopeses' were definitely on the rise. Louisa felt a surge of satisfaction that she'd been the instrument of their good fortune.

Now, as Mr. Scopes plied the knocker with a proprietary air and young Jem and his great-aunt grinned at one another in delight, Louisa's spirits began to lift. She was back in Bath, a place where she'd been happy. And even if the circumstances had changed drastically, who was to say that she could not be so again?

Mr. Scopes's knock was soon answered by the landlady herself, a short, roly-poly woman dressed all in black. "Oh, are you the actors?" she inquired, pronouncing the final word as if it might be interchangeable with "Hottentot." She stared at Miss Nell Scopes in some alarm—brought on, perhaps, by the bright green turban with sprigs of orange hair sticking out from under it, or perhaps by the lady's theatrical smile, made no less disarming by its lack of teeth. The landlady seemed somewhat reassured, however, by Mr. Scopes's air of down-at-the-heels respectability and Jem's shy, engaging grin. Finally, she was quite relieved by Louisa's ladylike appearance. She opened the door wide and ushered them into the house, explaining in a flurried tone that they were her first lodgers, that she'd never expected to be reduced to such a circumstance, that "dear Mr. Bottoms has just recently passed away—and well—it does seem sinful not to offer accommodations with Bath so full and all." However, they must simply consider themselves to be "paying guests." She put much more emphasis on "paying," though, Louisa noted with an inward smile, than she had placed on "guests."

Aunt Nell's stage-trained ear caught the inflection, too. "She's heard that all actors go out their windows in the middle of the night, I shouldn't wonder," the actress said in an aside.

The four trooped behind Mrs. Bottoms up the stairs to the first floor, where the landlady assigned them rooms. With a sigh of relief for the cleanliness of her chamber and the apparent comfort of the four-poster bed, Louisa disposed of the few possessions she'd brought along and settled into Trim Street.

In spite of her resolution to put all snobbery firmly in the past where it belonged, it took some effort on Louisa's part next morning to accept with any sort of grace Aunt Nell's invitation to visit the famous Pump Room right away. "I can't wait to drink the water and grow myself some brand-new teeth." The lady gave her impish grin, and Louisa's class barriers were pushed aside by a surge of affection for the redoubtable old lady. So much for exploring on her own. It was better, anyhow, she concluded, not to relive the past. And after all, what did it matter if heads turned their way to stare at the exotic old theatrical bird with her bright orange plumage. Louisa had no credit to maintain. Besides, she was an actress and should become accustomed to being stared at.

Still she could not prevent herself from choosing her most conservative gray walking dress and a plain bonnet of unbleached straw for the expedition. Aunt Nell looked her up and down critically as she joined the old lady in the hall. "You're too drab by half for an actress, dearie," was the final verdict. "But never mind. You'll get an eye for color yet. It comes with the feel you get for drama."

Louisa's eyes opened wide at the dramatic proof Miss Nell Scopes offered for her thesis. The bright green turban was once more perched upon the orange hair, but she'd added a yellow plume that waved above it in a gaudy arc. Her royal purple walking dress was tamboured liberally with yellow. Kid gloves and slippers were sunny yellow too. It occurred to Louisa that she herself just might become invisible, eclipsed as it were by so much radiance.

Already quite bedazzled by her companion, Louisa stepped forth into the glare of Bath. She had forgotten how the city could sparkle in the rays of a midsummer sun. Much of its architectural elegance came from the pale golden stone that served as a reflector. And its granite-squared pavements, washed clean by a rain shower that had come and gone during the night, possessed a similar quality. All in all, between the combined brilliance of Miss Scopes and their environment, Louisa felt herself in some danger of being blinded. She wondered with a barely suppressed giggle if, for safety, she should not view them through smoked glass.

The Pump Room, though seemingly a bit smaller now, surpassed in elegance Louisa's childhood memories. She had probably had too little architectural appreciation at that point, she thought, to be conscious of the pleasing proportions of the room with its Corinthian three-quarter columns placed at intervals all along the walls, interspersed occasionally by alcoves that gave added grace and variety to the scheme while enshrining the mineral-water fountain, the famous Tompion Clock, and the statue of Beau Nash.

As usual, the room was crowded with summer visitors, the business of taking the waters being for the most part only an excuse to congregate and swap the latest *on dits* of gossip concerning the people of note now in Bath and the latest scandal in London.

But despite the throngs, Louisa noted as she and Miss Scopes paused in the entryway to get their bearings, heads still turned their way.

"Well, best take our medicine first and get it over with." With her actress's instincts aroused, Aunt Nell saw the effect she was creating and built on it as she swept across the room toward the fountain alcove in a manner that would have done Covent Garden proud. Louisa trailed along behind, slapping down the impulse to turn tail and run as people stared, eyebrows rose, chins dropped, and ladies tittered behind fans to mark their progress.

"Ugh!" Miss Scopes pronounced at the initial sip, reminding Louisa suddenly of her father's first reaction to the healthful waters. "Well, anything that tastes this bad is bound to be good for you in the long run," Miss Scopes added with her own particular brand of cheerfulness, erasing the comparison.

The actress ran a professional eye over the Pump Room while she sipped noisily. "We ain't likely to draw from here," was her pronouncement. "Too many swells."

Louisa, who had also been surveying the crowd, but furtively, afraid of spotting some acquaintance in the crush, almost voiced her relief aloud. "You're perfectly right," was all she said, however. "I imagine these people never venture beyond the Theatre Royal."

Bath's Theatre Royal was one of only a handful of government-licensed theaters in the provinces. The luminaries of the London stage performed there, whereas the likes of the Scopes players had to content themselves with makeshift premises and present their plays as "free" performances sandwiched in between concerts and the like that could legally be charged for.

Aunt Nell evidently thought Louisa's comment cloaked regret. "Don't worry, love," she said. "You'll play the Royal yet. And London, too, or I miss my guess," she added for good measure.

Taking their cue from the other promenaders, they strolled around a bit. Then Miss Scopes declared her intention of "drinking one more glass of the vile bilge for good measure" before they left. Louisa, however, declined the treat and was staring up at the sculptor's representation of the uncrowned King of Bath, Beau Nash, when a voice behind her made her gasp and clutch at a chair for support. The words were ordinary enough. "I'm waiting for Miss Sedgwick. You know what women are. She doubtlessly spotted a bonnet in a shop window on the way." So it was not the message spoken but the tone and timbre of the voice that caused Louisa's scalp to prickle and made the blood drain from her face. Adrian! She did not believe in ghosts, but still—

Louisa wheeled and stared around her. There was nothing to account for what she thought she'd heard. Some trick of the imagination, without a doubt. Possibly she was more fatigued by travel than she had realized. But then the voice spoke again, this time commenting lazily on the likelihood of rain, and she gazed wildly about and tracked it to its source—Lord Lyston!

Louisa drew in her breath sharply at the sight of the tall, harsh-featured, dark-haired, hard-muscled baron. He was dressed conservatively but elegantly in a dark blue double-breasted long-tailed riding coat, tight biscuit-colored breeches, and gleaming riding boots, and he stood a few yards from her talking to a foppish older man.

Even now that the mystery was explained, Louisa was still shaken. She had not noticed when they'd met in Brussels that this hateful stranger was possessed of Adrian's voice. She had noted the eyes, of course. But the stronger facets of Lyston's personality had completely overshadowed this second resemblance to his younger brother. It was only when she'd heard him speak—disembodied, as it were—that the similarity became impossible to miss.

Louisa struggled to compose herself and was planning her escape route when Lord Lyston must have felt her stare. The bored gaze shifted from his companion's face and settled upon hers. There was one instant of frowning puzzlement before recognition came. Then the deep blue eyes narrowed, and Louisa fairly quailed before their flash of hatred.

Oh, dear God, Lord Lyston! How could she possibly have forgotten that the Grayson family seat was here in Somerset! From the look of him, the baron must have ridden into Bath. Her eyes dropped in confusion before his hateful glare, but as she turned her back to him hastily and continued her appraisal of Beau Nash, she could still feel his hard stare boring into her.

Louisa was rejoined shortly by Miss Nell Scopes, whose tooth-scarce mouth was pursed into a grimace of distaste for the mineral water she'd just drunk. As Louisa hurried the astonished actress from the room, she glanced nervously toward Lord Lyston, but saw with relief that he was no longer looking in her direction. He had been joined by a stylish, rather attractive lady near his own age— the elusive Miss Sedgwick he'd spoken of, no doubt. Indeed, as predicted, she did hold a hatbox in her hand. The lady was gazing coquettishly up into his lordship's eyes, talking rapidly with a great deal of animation. Unfortunately Lord Lyston did not appear captivated by her conversation. This became evident as he turned his attention from the flirting woman to watch Louisa through narrowed eyes as she self-consciously propelled Miss Nell on past him. Louisa, for her part, gave him just one more quick, nervous glance. But that was quite enough. She could not possibly have missed, even in so short a time, the menace in his stare.

That night, in the solitude of her room, before blowing out her candle and dropping off to sleep, Louisa skimmed the pages of her landlady's *Bath Herald* idly. The betrothal notice of the Honourable

Letitia Sedgwick to Richard Grayson, sixth Baron Lyston, leaped out at her. As she read it carefully for the second time, Louisa realized that she was certain of two things. First, she had made a powerful enemy in Lord Lyston; and second, he was not at all in love with the lady whom he planned to make his wife.

Chapter Six

NELL SCOPES HAD BEEN CORRECT WHEN SHE'D PRE-
dicted that the swells would stay away from
their performance. And so, initially, did the majority of the hoi polloi. This was in spite of all the
handbills Mr. Bennett had circulated around the
town advertising the arrival of an "internationally
famous troupe fresh from their triumph on the
Continent."

Mr. Scopes had decided that it might be prudent
to rest Shakespeare for a bit. And so they opened
with Hannah More's popular tragedy, *Percy*, with
Mr. Draper cast in the title role and Mrs. Grayson
playing the female lead. At first the audience had
been merely lukewarm toward the play, tolerating
it as a penance to be paid in order to view the pantomime that followed. However, they had warmed
up considerably each time Louisa came onstage.
Though not nearly so unruly as the Brussels audience, they seemed to share the same opinion: the

Scopes Company had little on the whole to recommend it, but there was something extraordinary about its newest player. When the dramatic portion of the program finally limped to its conclusion, it was therefore followed by a great deal more applause than it deserved.

Backstage Mr. Bennett seemed reasonably satisfied with his investment. Or at least he was willing to accept Mr. Scopes's alibis for the production's weak points. He seemed to understand that they'd had to recruit last-minute substitutes to take the place of lost professionals who, for whatever reason, had not bothered to join their fellow players there in Bath. He accepted the fact that there had not been time to rehearse sufficiently—that Mrs. Grayson was a novice—but, Mr. Scopes assured him, all would soon come right.

"Oh, I'm not concerned about Mrs. Grayson." Mr. Bennett, overweight, sixty if a day, leered lasciviously. The whole company was crowded together in one dressing room, removing makeup, changing clothes, making sure their costumes were ready for the next performance. Louisa had retired modestly behind a screen to take off her dress, and, in deference to her star status, hand it over to Old Nell. She now wore a pale pink frilled-silk dressing gown and was seated before a mirror taking off her makeup. Right behind her, Mr. Draper, having either despaired of—or scorned—his turn behind the screen, changed his breeches with a true actor's lack of concern for the prudish conventions of ordinary folk.

"No, indeed." Mr. Bennett patted Louisa on the shoulder with a sweaty palm and leered once more. "I'm not worried about this little lady coming up to scratch. Now it's true she did seem to be making a few speeches up as she went along." He chuckled.

"But what's that got to say to anything next to the fact the audience loved her? The public! Yes, indeed, Mrs. Grayson, the public! They're the ones to look to. Forget the critics. It's the audience that knows what's what. And tonight they recognized a real performer—someone destined to be one of the great artists of the stage."

"Fustian!" A dry, familiar voice spoke behind Louisa. She raised her eyes in the mirror to see Lord Lyston standing there. "The audience recognized an extraordinarily pretty woman. That is all. Her performance would have been laughed right out of Drury Lane."

"Now, look here, sir!"

"How dare you, sir!"

Mr. Bennett and Mr. Scopes protested simultaneously, but Lord Lyston's eyes never left Louisa's reflected face. With a great effort of will, she slapped down her anger, gave him a level stare, then returned her attention to the business of cleaning off her makeup.

"Where may I speak to you privately, Mrs. Varley?" he demanded curtly, completely ignoring the bluster all around him. Indeed, Mr. Bennett and Mr. Scopes had begun backing away nervously, obviously intimidated by his lordship's air of consequence. Even Old Nell, after one belligerent "Now, see 'ere, your nibs," had been sent scurrying across the room by a frosty glance.

Louisa, however, felt no such intimidation. She deliberately took her time before replying. That Lord Lyston detested her heartily was evident. Well, she felt no cordiality toward him, when it came to that.

"I need to talk to you, Mrs. Varley," he repeated.

"Mrs. Grayson," she corrected him with cool detachment. "And I see no reason for us to talk. If you wish to finish your review of my performance, I assure you it will not be necessary. My own critical faculties are better than you may suppose."

Lord Lyston was growing angry. "You know damn well why I wish to speak to you!" he snapped, but lowered his voice even as he did so. "Don't try to pretend you didn't expect to see me. You recognized me in the Pump Room the other day."

Louisa stood and turned to face him. "You are quite mistaken. I did not expect to see you. I make it a strict rule never to meet my public after a performance. Now, if you'll excuse me." She started to walk past him toward the screen. However, he grabbed her by the arm with a grip that made her flinch.

"You'll talk to me or to my solicitor," he said between clenched teeth. "And I think you'd be well advised to make it me. He's far more parsimonious with my blunt than I'm inclined to be. But one way or another, I intend to stop you from dragging my brother's name through the mire. So now if you want to turn some of that famous charm on me that you used to entrap poor, naïve Adrian, who knows—I might even make it worth your while to leave this flea-bitten troupe."

Louisa slapped him, then—hard across the cheek. The sound reverberated through the dressing room, causing everyone else to drop all pretense of not watching them and stare open-mouthed. But no one present was more horrified than Louisa.

For a moment, she thought Lord Lyston might strike her back. His face contorted with rage as he clenched his fists until his knuckles whitened. She almost wished he would retaliate. She wanted him to lose composure just as she had. She railed at herself silently for having done so.

But "Very theatrical" was Lyston's only comment.

"Now that's out of your system, I repeat, where can we go to talk? Don't try it, actor—or is it actress? I warn you, you can only regret the impulse."

Since the last remark was directed across her shoulder, and since Lord Lyston had released her arm to meet another challenge, Louisa wheeled around. Young Jem Scopes had picked up a stage prop sword and was advancing to her rescue. Louisa did not quite know whether to laugh or cry, he looked so ludicrous. Much against his will, he had been pressed into a female walk-on part. And although he had removed his lady's wig, his face was thick with paint, and he kept tripping over his long skirt as he advanced to meet the enemy. Hastily, Louisa stepped between Lord Lyston and her rescuer, noting at the same time that his lordship's anger was becoming diffused by an obvious desire to laugh. "It's all right, Jem," she said. "The gentleman is leaving."

Trying to disguise relief in a belligerent glare that augured well for his future on the stage, Jem put down his sword. Then, for the first time he recalled the dress he wore. His two bright rouge spots disappeared in a matching surge of red as he began to yank off the odious garment.

"You do have quite a way with halflings, haven't you?" Lord Lyston remarked to Louisa underneath his breath. "Is that Adrian's successor?"

"Lord Lyston, I was prepared to offer an apology for striking you just now. But you've reminded me that I could hardly help myself. Now, will you leave, or shall I have you thrown out? Even though Master Scopes is no match for you, I'm sure there are sufficient stagehands here to do the job."

"That I doubt. But since you seem determined to be obstinate, I will let my solicitor deal with you. And warn him first not to be hoodwinked by that angelic face into believing a word you say. 'I've no intention of marrying your brother, Lord Lyston,'" he mimicked, forcing her to recall the painful details of their first meeting. Louisa opened her mouth to explain the circumstances of her breach of faith, then realized how impossible that would be. This man would never understand. Black was black and white was white with him.

"I'm not sure what sort of part you're playing, actress," Lyston continued, "but keep one thing in mind: I owe you nothing."

Then he turned abruptly and left while Louisa sank weakly down into her chair and picked up her face cream with hands that showed a deplorable tendency to shake.

Next morning, when Mrs. Bottoms, the landlady, came bustling into her bedchamber with the news that a gentleman was waiting to speak with her, Louisa sighed. Lord Lyston had wasted no time, it seemed, in sending round his solicitor. But when she entered the withdrawing room a little later, it was Lyston himself who waited there.

He was dressed in the same riding clothes she'd seen him wearing in the Pump Room and was walking around the room impatiently. He stopped his pacing to look her up and down.

Suddenly Louisa regretted that she had not quizzed Mrs. Bottoms more particularly about her caller and, as a consequence, taken more trouble with her toilette. Her sprigged muslin dress with its ribbon sash just underneath the bust and its ruffle of lace just underneath the chin seemed deplorably unsophisticated. Lord Lyston evidently thought so, too. "How old are you?" he asked abruptly.

Louisa looked at him coldly, not deigning to reply.

"No wonder Adrian was taken in. You look no older than he, though I happen to know you're nearer thirty."

"I'm twenty-three," Louisa was goaded into saying, then could have bitten off her tongue as Lyston laughed nastily.

"Lord Lyston, I don't know why you have come here when I made it plain last night that we've nothing whatsoever to say to one another. Actors do not keep the same hours as other folk. Now, since you have roused me from my bed, at least do endeavor to be civil. I have the headache and propose to have a cup of tea and breakfast. You may wait here until I finish, or join me in the dining room, just as you wish." With that she swept out of the room, leaving him little choice but to follow her.

Louisa seated herself at the head of Mrs. Bottoms's pillar-and-claw dining table and indicated with a gesture that Lord Lyston should occupy the place opposite at the foot. "I think not," he said coolly, pulling out the chair next to hers. "I don't intend to shout."

He stared around him at the small but pleasantly appointed room with its view of a tiny garden that fairly burst its bounds with roses. He made no comment, though, as Mrs. Bottoms's maid, obviously as flustered as her mistress by a visit from such a nob, scurried around piling mounds of ham, boiled eggs, rolls, and orange marmalade on the table. "My God, what does she think we are?" His lordship's eyes widened at the abundance.

"There are others in the household to be fed," Louisa murmured, pouring out tea for both of them and suppressing a desire to giggle at their cozy domestic scene. She stole a sideways look at the scowling, almost-handsome face of the Baron Lyston, assessed the quality of his tailoring—Weston

72

of London without a doubt—took in the arrogant consequence of his bearing, and, to her horror, felt a twinge of regret for a way of life she'd tossed away so carelessly. Regret vanished quickly, though, as Lord Lyston addressed the maid who had reappeared. "You, there—see to it we are not disturbed."

Louisa sighed as she handed him his steaming cup. "I can only hope that your imperiousness doesn't cause me to lose my lodgings. They are not easily come by for actresses, you know."

"Probably not. But you can explain that my visit isn't likely to be repeated." He spread a roll liberally with marmalade and took a bite that would have caused his governess to wince if she still lived. "We'd best get down to business before that young fool with the dress and sword decides to play knight errant and ride to your rescue again." Lyston suddenly grinned at the recollection while Louisa noted with surprise that he was capable of looking almost pleasant. It didn't last. "How much do you want?" he asked abruptly.

"I don't know what you mean."

"Of course you do. How much do I have to pay to hush you up about the sham marriage you went through with my brother? And to stop you from dragging his name through the mud as you're doing now."

Louisa's cup rattled deplorably upon its saucer. "Lord Lyston," she began, but he interrupted.

"I've decided to make you an allowance for life. I'm prepared to double what Bennett's paying you. I realize that your earning power could exceed that amount for a year or so. For, as I pointed out last night, though you're short on talent, no one would deny your extraordinary beauty. So you should do well as long as it lasts." He held up his hand again as she tried to interrupt. "No, hear me out. I'm offering you rather more than a competence. Which, by the by, would greatly exceed any legal claim you could make even if your marriage were declared valid, as I assure you it would not be. Believe it—Adrian had little property of his own. He was almost totally dependent upon me. Oh, yes, one more important point. The allowance would not stop upon the occasion of your marriage. And you're bound to bring some poor devil up to scratch." He sneered. "Not likely another with Adrian's pedigree, but one of these new mill-owning nabobs could make your fortune. And I would, in fact, welcome—not penalize—such an event. Might even provide a bonus, in point of fact. Now, have you any questions?"

"Yes, just one. Why have you chosen to behave so despicably toward me?"

"You term it despicable? Most would call it handsome."

Despite her efforts to steady it, Louisa's voice shook with rage. "You have no right to insult me in this way. I have asked nothing of you, nor have I publicized my marriage to Adrian."

"Oh, but you will."

"You mistake the matter. Now, if you'll excuse me, we have excluded the others from their breakfast long enough."

"No, you'll not run away again." Lyston grabbed Louisa's wrist as she started to leave the table. "And you can drop the fine-lady role with me. I know your past history only too well. As for your not wanting anything from me, why else the sudden rush to Bath from Brussels? And as for not publicizing your marriage, why else the use of the Grayson name when you've so many others to choose from?" His eyes blazed in anger, now, and her own ignited.

"My coming to Bath was a mere happenstance. Which you may believe or not." She took note of his derisive laugh. "What you think of me bothers me not at all. As for my use of the Grayson name, I made a solemn promise to do so." Her voice broke and he laughed softly again, mocking what he obviously thought was a performance. Louisa stifled the urge to throw tea in his hateful face and proceeded calmly. "As I said, what you may think of me is not the issue. Now I really must insist that you excuse me."

He was still holding her wrist and his grip tightened. "Not until you accept my terms."

"Then we are bound together in this ridiculous position for life. I shall never do that."

They glared at one another for several seconds. Lord Lyston finally acknowledged the impasse and released his grip. "It seems I've no other recourse," he said, "than to go to law and force you to drop my brother's name."

"I doubt you can to that," Louisa replied steadily. "Oh, you may annul the marriage, but an actress is free to use any name she chooses. And despite your jealous possessiveness, 'Grayson' is hardly as notable as 'Hanover.' No one is likely to connect it with your family unless you raise the issue."

"Why do you choose to dishonor Adrian? He must have cared for you." Lord Lyston's arrogance had slipped a little. Louisa saw true pain in his eyes as he spoke of his dead brother.

"I have no intention of dishonoring Adrian," she replied more softly than she might have before noting that bit of vulnerability. "I shall continue to use the name, because I promised. But, as I said, there is no need to connect the name to him." Then she rose to her feet. "I think you can find your own way out."

"You convinced me of your good faith once. You're not likely to again. I don't know what sort of game you hope to play. But if you think to move in at Graylands, disenchant yourself. It will never happen. Good day, Mrs. Varley."

Lyston had thrown his napkin down upon the table to stride across the room and jerk wide the door before Louisa felt compelled to call after him. "Lord Lyston."

"Yes?" He turned scowling, one hand upon the knob.

"Have you had any word of Private Webster?"

"I beg your pardon?"

"Private Samuel Webster. I understand he was employed at Graylands. Have you had news of him?"

He paused a moment before answering. "As a matter of fact, I have. He was killed at Waterloo."

"Oh, no!" she breathed. He stood and watched as the tears brimmed into her eyes.

"Don't tell me that Sam was one of your conquests, too."

The words were intended to be an insult, but Louisa no longer cared. "Yes, I rather think he was," she answered softly.

Lord Lyston gave her a searching look, then closed the door behind him.

Chapter
Seven

*L*OUISA WENT BACK INTO HER BEDCHAMBER, AVOIDING the curious looks of the Scopes family coming down the stairs. It was obvious they were well aware of Lyston's visit.

She sat and wept a bit for Private Webster—at least she was convinced that was why she cried— and then resolutely pushed all thought of him to the back of her mind to be pulled out on some future date and mourned for properly, along with the other sadnesses filed away there—the loss of a father's love, a marriage turned to a mockery, and the death of Adrian.

She had piled up a lot of grief, she thought as a wave of self-pity washed over her—for twenty-three years of life, or even for the thirty that Lord Lyston took her for. Then cleansing anger erased self-pity at the thought of Lyston. She walked over to the washstand and splashed her face repeatedly with cold water. But just as she was making progress with her repairs, the vision of Private Webster returned to undo what she'd accomplished. "Master Adrian wouldn't have married you if you wasn't quality," he had said. Why couldn't Lord Lyston have the same faith in his brother's judgment? Well, that was his lordship's problem, she thought bitterly, splashing her face once more, then resolutely picking up a copy of her script to go over and over those lines she had stumbled on the night before.

Hard work, she found, was a classic antidote for being blue-deviled. Louisa insisted upon extra rehearsal before the next performance. The rest of the cast grumbled—wasn't appearing three nights a week enough?—and Mr. Scopes himself had been less than enthusiastic. But he had given in and had scheduled time from Mr. Bennett when the other acts engaged there were not busy on the stage.

When Louisa noted a slight improvement in the next performance, she felt justified in all her pushing. And she felt even more justified as the house attendance increased gradually, both in numbers and in the quality of the patrons. Once while declaiming a particularly impassioned speech straight toward the audience, she even thought she spied Lord Lyston sitting there. But afterward, when she'd steeled herself for a backstage confrontation and he had not appeared, she judged herself mistaken. She chalked up the illusion to her growing tendency to see him everywhere, so strong was the impression he'd made.

As promised, Lyston sent his man of business to see her. But contrary to his lordship's threats, Louisa had found it far simpler to deal with this gentleman than with his employer. After only a short conversation in the Trim Street drawing room, conducted with reasonableness and courtesy on both sides, the lawyer, a spare, dry-looking little man in his late fifties, seemed more than willing to accept Louisa's continued insistence that she wished nothing from his lordship and had no desire to put forward any claim as his brother's wife. She refused point-blank the lawyer's echo of Lyston's offer of an allowance. But on the question of a name change, Mr. Spenser found her less than reasonable. No, she definitely would not discontinue using "Grayson" for her stage name. But here, too, the lawyer was willing to concede that the name was not his lordship's exclusive property and that the general public was not likely to make any connection unless Lyston made the mistake of drawing attention to the relationship. All in all, the lawyer seemed to know a stalemate when he saw it, and he parted on amicable terms with his client's adversary.

And that, Louisa hoped, was that. But she remained uneasy. For she recognized in Lord Lyston a soulmate to her father, a man totally accustomed to having his own way.

She was therefore braced for trouble when she arrived home from the theater late one night to find Mrs. Bottoms waiting up for her. "A letter came for you this afternoon, m'dear." Obviously the landlady was consumed by curiosity as she handed Louisa what might just as well have been left on a hall tray or slipped underneath her door. But when Louisa saw a crest indented into the sealing wax she understood why the landlady was so bug-eyed. But Mrs. Bottoms was doomed to disappointment. Louisa merely thanked her, excused herself, and went into her room to light a candle and break open the missive. Two pieces of cardboard spilled out upon the floor. She held the heavy notepaper toward the candle flame. "I think it's time you discovered what real acting is" was written in a bold black scrawl and signed simply "Richard Grayson."

Louisa picked up two Theatre Royal tickets and saw they were for the following Wednesday night. The play was to be *Macbeth*, starring John Philip Kemble and his sister, Mrs. Siddons, whom some critics called the greatest Lady Macbeth the stage had ever seen.

At first Louisa was so enraged that she barely stopped herself from sticking the tickets in the candle flame. There was no doubt in her mind now. Lyston had been present in her audience when she'd thought so. And he had taken sufficient trouble to discover what night she was not engaged to play. Box seats as well! There was also no doubt in her mind that Lyston had meant his gesture as an insult. He wished to infuriate her, and he had. But he'd also underestimated her professionalism. She, too, wished to see what real acting was.

Louisa placed the tickets carefully on the mantlepiece. She would attend the Royal and watch *Macbeth* from Lord Lyston's box. And she'd take Aunt Nell along to keep her company.

Nell Scopes was transported by the opportunity. "Sarah Siddons! Mercy me. You're actually asking me to go see Sarah Siddons? Bless me! I ain't set eyes on her since she played the Northern Circuit for Tate Wilkinson—back in the seventies, it was— and I don't mind saying she wasn't half an actress then, m'dear. Why, I could act rings around her myself, I don't mind saying, and was better-looking, too, if you can believe it—had a full set of teeth then, mind you. Poor Sarah'd flopped in London already, don't you know. The critics all but ran her out of town. But she was a learner. I'll hand her that. And you keep her example well in mind, Louisa. It's little wonder she's coming back to Bath.

She owes it to the place. She learned her craft right here. That's how she was able to finally make it back to London. Sarah Siddons! What I wouldn't give to see Sarah Siddons on the stage again!"

But it seemed that what she wouldn't give was the price of a box seat. Even when Louisa explained they were being treated, she wasn't overly impressed.

"By that nob you walloped in the dressing room on opening night?" she queried shrewdly. When Louisa nodded, she gave a disapproving snort. "Too high in the instep by half, that one is. I wouldn't of had to be born yesterday to realize that, first thing I set me glims on him. What's he up to anyhow? Offer you a *carte blanche*, did he?"

"Certainly not!" Louisa almost giggled at the thought.

"Well, he'll get around to it. Mark my words. That kind's never up to any good, and you'd best remember it. And a lovely young actress like you—why, these gentry-coves all think it's some kind of game to be played, like chasing down a poor little mite of a fox. It's a wonder they don't wear their pink coats and carry horse whips when they come back stage. Come to think on it, that one was on horseback when he came here. Well, at least he's honest." She cackled appreciatively at her wit. "Now don't look so Friday-faced, young missy. Of course I spied on you. If I don't keep an eye on you, who will, I ask you? And that villain's ready to unleash his dogs just any minute and come after you yelling 'view halloo,' you mark my words."

But if Louisa thought Miss Nell had gone off course to the point of forgetting the ticket prices, she couldn't have been more wrong. The actress had a great deal more to say about the sinful extravagance of paying seven shillings for the same play that could be seen in the gallery for two.

"But Miss Nell, we aren't paying it," Louisa pointed out.

" 'Tis sinful all the same. Especially"—the old woman cut her eyes craftily toward Louisa—"when you stop and think as how four folk could get the benefit of what only two can see."

"Oh." The light began to dawn. "Mr. Scopes and Jem!" And suddenly it struck her as being rather a good idea to turn Lord Lyston's insulting gift into a theater party for four seedy players. Even though the company's fortunes were on the rise, what with Mrs. Bottoms's rent and all the expenses of production, the Scopeses weren't able to finance this kind of treat. Nell saw Louisa begin to waver and pressed home her advantage. "Let me change the tickets for you, love."

"Very well, then," Louisa capitulated. "But not the gallery, mind you. I want to see the Siddons and Kemble facial expressions. I'm there to learn, remember?"

But it was plain by the concentration on her face that Miss Nell Scopes was still busy doing sums that involved the difference in the price of the gallery and the pit. Louisa cut the old lady's subtraction short by pretending to change her mind and opting for the box seats after all. Shocked out of her latest attempt at thrift, Miss Scopes snatched up the tickets and promised to exchange them for four in the pit. "The minute the box office opens at ten on Wednesday morning."

When Wednesday evening finally arrived, Louisa's excitement caught her quite off guard. While dressing, she almost convinced herself that it was merely professional anticipation she was feeling. What aspiring actress would not wish to see the top actors of her chosen field? But then Louisa admitted honestly that the prospect of an evening out was causing most of her exhilaration. She had not had a social engagement for a long, long time. Not since the Duchess of Richmond's ball, in fact, and that could hardly count as a gala evening. At no time, though, did she allow herself to think that the possibility of seeing Lord Lyston at the play had any appeal for her.

Louisa's enthusiasm was dampened by the sight of the others in her party. They had gathered in Mrs. Bottoms's drawing room to join that lady in a glass of ratafia before proceeding to the theater. The male Scopeses were not too bad, Louisa thought. She was quite surprised to find them wearing knee smalls, but, then, she'd overlooked their access to Mr. Bennett's costumes. Their dark coats and white knee breeches were obviously never tailored for them—or for anyone near their size, when it came to that. But still, if one were not overcritical, they looked respectable. And Louisa managed to suppress a smile at the height of Master Jem's shirt points while she fervently hoped he'd have no desire to turn his head before the night was through.

But it was Miss Nell Scopes who forced Louisa to fight against hysteria. If she had thought the lady's taste bizarre before, it was only because she had never seen Miss Scopes rise to the challenge of an evening on the town. Bright yellow was the color chosen for her gown. It, too, Louisa guessed, was by courtesy of the theater and designed for someone forty years the wearer's junior. The material was Italian taffeta, the bodice low enough to overexpose her sagging breasts and crepy skin. The hemline, edged with pointed lace, unkindly called attention to the ankles which hardly needed the extra emphasis, entwined as they were by the orange satin ribbons of Miss Nell's slippers. But it was the plumage of this bird of paradise that caused Louisa's chin to drop. That Aunt Nell had found three orange ostrich feathers of the exact same shade as her brilliant hair defied all the laws of probability. But discover them she had, and they fanned out above her forehead like some nightmare fleur-de-lis. For a wild moment, Louisa considered feigning the headache and fleeing to her room.

But Miss Nell Scopes was not enchanted with Louisa's appearance, either. Louisa warily watched Miss Nell sip ratafia with noisy disapproval while the old actress looked her critically up and down. Never one to keep her opinion to herself, Miss Nell soon pronounced her verdict. "I don't mind saying, m'dear, if you plan to make your living on the stage you're going to have to pay your looks a bit more mind."

Jem, who had been stealing covert glances at Louisa, glared disapprovingly at his great-aunt. "What do you mean? Louisa looks smashing. Top of the trees!" He blushed at his presumption.

"Humph. Too drab by half. No flair at all," was the professional's verdict. "How do you expect to stand out in that ensemble?" she asked accusingly.

Louisa looked down at her pale blue satin ball dress with its covering of spider gauze and started to protest that the last thing she desired was to "stand out." But on second thought, she kept her silence.

"I've got some feathers I can lend you," Aunt Nell went on. "Blood-red 'uns. Brighten you up a lot."

"Uh, no, thank you," Louisa hastily replied.

"They'd beat those pearl things all to pieces. Who's going to see pearls in your fair hair?" Louisa had coiffed her locks in the Grecian style and entwined a rope of artificial pearls among the curls.

"Louisa looks like a lady," Jem pronounced.

"She'd best look like an actress," was his aunt's rejoinder.

They all left Trim Street in time to walk leisurely to the Theatre Royal and arrived at half-past six, just as it opened, and the fashionable were emerging from their sedan chairs, the accepted mode of transportation for Bath, whose hilliness made carriages impractical. "Looks like a sellout." Mr. Scopes blinked at the crowd surging toward the entrance and could not keep the envy from his voice.

As the four of them found seats on the benches in the pit, Louisa felt a rush of surprised gratitude for the thrift that had driven Aunt Nell to make their ticket switch. Here, though some of the illusion might be lost as they sat close enough to observe the lines of makeup, they'd not miss a single nuance of expression. And though there was no doubt that the Siddons-Kemble voices would find their way to the recesses of the gallery, still, here they'd get full benefit.

As the theater filled, Louisa at first enjoyed gazing around her. For though the Quality might predominate, all strata of Bath society were represented on this night, drawn irresistibly by the pull of the famous stars. But then she discovered that far too many patrons were looking back. She and her companions were the object of considerable attraction, even in the midst of the crowded pit.

"Some of your public is here, m'dear," Aunt Nell whispered in a voice whose carrying power the great Mrs. Siddons would be hard-pressed to beat. "You're being noticed." Louisa suppressed a giggle. She knew quite well which one of them was creating all the stir.

She stole a glance behind her fan at the box they should have occupied and found that it was filled, though she failed to recognize any of the occupants. Well, she'd hardly expected Lord Lyston to send her tickets for a box he himself would share. Indeed, on second thought, she doubted that he'd even attend the theater on the night she was due to do so. But she soon found she was mistaken on that count. Just before the curtain rose, an empty stage box began to fill, and she spied Lord Lyston in the group of elegantly clad members of the *ton*, among whom she recognized Miss Sedgwick, his fiancée. Louisa smiled to herself as she saw him glance across the way to the box he'd reserved for her. His expression did not change, of course, but she hoped he thought his bit of petty malice had misfired. She also hoped that he'd not discover them, a circumstance she'd have relied upon if it were not for her companion's conspicuous plumage. Baron Lyston was not likely to seek acquaintances in the pit.

But as the curtain rose Louisa forgot about Lord Lyston—and indeed all else as Shakespeare's spell was evoked with a skill she'd never imagined possible.

It was, of course, the leading lady, not the famous brother, that her attention fastened on. Louisa held her breath each time the actress spoke. Much of the "brilliant beauty" the critics once acclaimed was faded now. "She's sixty if she's a day," Aunt Nell had whispered audibly on the star's first entrance. But Mrs. Siddons's figure was still good, her carriage graceful, her features striking. It was the latter that Louisa envied most—the Roman nose, the heavy brows, all those larger-than-life attributes so suited for the stage. And she marveled at Mrs. Siddons's versatility, both of expression and of voice. The aging player could turn from melting tenderness to chilling horror in mere seconds. "Lord Lyston was right," Louisa despaired as she weighed herself in the balance of the Siddons genius and came up wanting. "I am not an actress. And I never will be."

When the curtain came down for the interval, Louisa was left spellbound by the tragedy unfolding on the stage. The same could not be said of her more seasoned friends. "My bottom's numb, let's walk," Miss Scopes proclaimed loudly while Master Scopes pulled some nuts from the recesses of a pocket and began to crack them with resounding pops. "Do let's stretch our legs," Mr. Scopes agreed, and they joined the throngs filing out into the lobby.

"Humph!" Aunt Nell snorted. "We'll wind up smothered here." And before Louisa could protest, she headed out and up the stairs toward the tiers of boxes with Mr. Scopes and Jem trailing close behind. Reluctantly, Louisa followed them.

Aunt Nell was right. There was more room to breathe. Only a few of the box holders were strolling down the corridors. These gave the interlopers curious looks, mostly directed at the orange plumes, then passed on to chat with friends in other boxes. Louisa hugged the wall, trying to be as inconspicuous as possible in case some acquaintance from her former life should be among this elite section of the audience. Then, to her horror, she saw Lord Lyston's party emerge from their box door. Some of the gentlemen wished to "blow a cloud." Only when Lyston turned in quite the opposite direction with his back toward her and lighted his cheroot did Louisa start to breathe normally again.

Miss Sedgwick, however, faced her way, giving Louisa ample opportunity to observe Lord Lyston's fiancée. The lady looked as proud as he, she thought. And indeed, the young woman possessed an air of consequence well suited to his lordship's. In other ways, Louisa decided, they were a well-matched pair. They might have been a brother and a sister, she reflected, they looked so much alike—tall, dark-haired, blue-eyed—though the lady's eyes, unfortunately, lacked the vivid intensity of her fiancé's. For Lord Lyston's eyes were really quite remarkable, Louisa reflected rather generously, then went on to disqualify the compliment by deciding that the only reason she found them so attractive was that they were a characteristic once held in common with his younger brother. She continued to amuse herself by studying the little group, taking note of the fortune in diamonds that the honorable Letitia wore around her neck, then watching with detached amusement that lady's seemingly futile attempt to captivate her fiancé.

Meanwhile Louisa's own companions were deep in a technical discussion of the play, dealing primarily with the number of witches and hobgoblins used in one scene that, Shakespeare notwithstanding, was really no more than a spectacular pantomime. Then just at the point when Nell Scopes's criticism was carrying the day over her more conservative male companions, the old actress happened to glance down the way and spy the group Louisa observed. "Why, there's Lord Lyston," she whooped in her stage voice, made even more carrying by Sarah Siddons's fresh example. And, to Louisa's horror, she went cruising down the corridor like a three-masted ship, with orange sails unfurled.

Lord Lyston had turned as the sound of his name projected toward him. He now watched the actress's approach with fascinated disbelief. Louisa quickly clapped her fan before her face but could not prevent herself from peering over it.

"Your lordship," Miss Nell was at her most charming, self-cast, undoubtedly, in the role of some stage dutchess. "I spied you standing here and could not wait to make it known to you how prodigiously we are enjoying tonight's drama." Louisa noted to her horrified delight that, whereas Lyston seemed to have recovered from the initial shock, his fiancée's mouth was still hanging open, for the first time, probably, in its aristocratic life.

"It was too, too kind of you to send us tickets," Aunt Nell continued, and Louisa saw the light of understanding dawn in Lyston's eyes. "You must of known that Sarah Siddons and I were colleagues in our youth, fellow thespians, students of the Bard." The actress waved her hand gracefully, a la Mrs. Siddons, to underscore the point.

Indeed, Aunt Nell had quite forgotten that she was not the intended recipient of his lordship's bounty as she continued to pour out her effusive gratitude. Louisa's emotional state changed rapidly from initial horror into an alarming bent toward gigging hysteria when she observed the appalled looks Lord Lyston was receiving from his companions while they edged away from the astounding creature who had him cornered. Miss Sedgwick, Louisa saw with mounting appreciation, seemed only inches from a classic fit of vapors.

"Now I guess you're wondering," Aunt Nell continued archly, tapping his lordship coyly on the sleeve of his impeccably tailored coat, "why we didn't make use of the box-seat tickets that you sent us."

"Not particularly." If his lordship's tone was meant to be dismissive, it missed the mark.

"Well I don't mind saying that Louisa wanted to."

And, with a broad gesture, Aunt Nell riveted the group's attention upon Louisa, who closed her eyes and prayed for the theater's collapse. "Why, here's Lord Lyston, Louisa," Miss Scopes called out. Louisa's first impulse was to turn and run. But with the example of Mrs. Siddons fresh in her own mind as well as in Miss Scopes's, she stopped her vigorous fanning and gave his lordship a dazzling smile. Well done, she congratulated herself silently, noting his startled look and Miss Sedgwick's rapid intake of breath. Their companions stared first at her, then at his lordship, and finally at one another knowingly.

"As I was saying," the oblivious Aunt Nell continued, "Louisa wanted to keep the box-seat tickets that you sent. But I thought it a sinful waste, besides wanting to see dear Sarah right up close. Lawks, how that woman's aged! But you folk really should try the pit sometime. You don't know what you're missing." She turned expansively toward Lyston's friends, who shrank away a little more.

"We'll look forward to that treat," Lord Lyston told her haughtily. "Now, if you'll excuse us." He turned back in the direction of his box.

"Oh, but you must give Louisa a chance to thank you, too." Aunt Nell seemed to have forgotten all her warnings against Lyston as she gave Weston's famous tailoring a tug.

"Another time, perhaps."

"Louisa!" As Aunt Nell's loud summons rang down the corridor, heads popped from box entrances like cuckoos from Black Forest clocks. "His lordship has to go now. You must thank him for the treat he's given us."

Louisa was almost too far gone now to reply. For she had finally succumbed and was collapsed against the wall in helpless, silent laughter. The blue eyes that she had found herself admiring a little while ago now met hers with haughty chilliness. Louisa sobered up immediately and mustered all the dignity at her command. Then, in her best imitation of Nell Scopes's voice and gesture, she gave his lordship an airy wave. "Thank 'ee ever so for the tickets, ducks," she called out shrilly.

His lordship stood a moment as though impaled. Then he bowed stiffly in her direction.

"Touché!" he said.

Chapter
Eight

*T*HE VISIT TO THE THEATRE ROYAL SEEMED THE BE-
ginning of an upward swing in Louisa's life.
Perhaps it was the superb example set for them
that inspired the Scopes performers with a new
surge of professionalism. Their rehearsals began
paying off. The small theater was filled almost every night they played. And if success also produced
a new problem for Louisa, a host of male admirers
of all ages and descriptions, their coarser advances
were rapidly disposed of by the strict chaperonage
of the Scopeses. Indeed, nothing could quell a libertine's advance quicker than a wrathful glare from
Miss Nell.

Another thing the Siddons-Kemble visit had accomplished was to show Louisa that, though it was
the exception and not the rule, an acting family
could attain respectability. She could only hope
that the male population of Bath had also noted
their example. Louisa began to feel more optimistic

about her future than she had felt since her first disastrous marriage. Though barred from that upper stratum of society she was born to, she still might manage middle-class respectability along with some measure of success in her chosen field. And if occasionally, when too fatigued by a performance to sleep, for instance, she felt a stir of rebellious discontent for all that was missing in her life, usually her days and nights were too involved with the business of the theater to allow any time for such futile, fruitless heart-burnings.

Another cause for quiet satisfaction was that between them, in the Theatre Royal confrontation, she and Aunt Nell had completely routed Baron Lyston. Louisa giggled wickedly as she recalled his starchy astonishment when cornered by the crone in the feathered crown. And now it appeared that he'd retired his troops and left the field to her. Whether he merely wished to avoid future embarrassment or whether his man of business had finally prevailed upon him to see the light of reason, Louisa could not know. She hoped, however, that he had come to realize that she posed no threat where he or his family honor was concerned.

And so Louisa began to feel a measure of contentment in her life and filled most of her days with rehearsal and performance and used the time when the Scopes troupe was not playing to explore Bath and the surrounding countryside. But it was the theater days she enjoyed the most, with the challenge of performance and the heady exhilaration of applause that made it all worthwhile.

Afterward she was always emotionally drained and enjoyed the leisurely walk from the theater on the outskirts of Bath to Trim Street. It was a chance to wind down keyed-up nerves, making it possible to fall to sleep in a reasonably short time.

Occasionally she and Aunt Nell walked together, but more often it was young Jem's duty to see her safely home while his great-aunt stayed on to make sure the costumes were hung properly and mended when the need arose.

Walking home with Louisa was a chore that Jeremiah Scopes usually looked forward to. But as they left the theater on a late summer's night, Louisa could sense Jem's sullen reluctance. She had seen him in a heated argument with his great-aunt a bit before and suspected he'd been trying to get out of the escort duty. Bone-tired though she was, Louisa increased her pace to try and rid him of the irksome chore as soon as possible.

Jem's face was quite morose there in the moonlight, and he walked with his hands rammed into his pockets and his head hung down. He was obviously deep in thought. As they approached a crossroads on the edge of town, he seemed to come to a decision. "Oh, I say, Louisa. Do you mind if we walk out of our way for just a bit?"

She did mind, but a pleading puppy-dog look stopped her protest. She even stifled the "Whatever for?" she'd been about to ask, and instead gave a weak smile of acquiescence and followed him.

They walked in quite the opposite direction from Trim Street and forever, it seemed to her, as Louisa despaired of ever seeing home again. Then finally they trudged through an open field toward a rudely constructed building, shedlike in everything but size. This structure was surrounded by vehicles of every kind—carts, wagons, carriages, sporting gigs—plus a wide assortment of horses that ranged from thoroughbred to plugs. Louisa looked longingly at the array, fancying even a dog cart in her weariness.

"I hope we ain't too late." Jem increased his pace while Louisa grabbed his arm.

"Too late for what? Jem, what is this place?"

He mumbled something unintelligible, and Louisa yanked once more. "Jeremiah Scopes, where are you taking me?"

"A rat pit," was the reluctant answer.

"A rat pit!" Louisa gasped. "Jem, how could you even consider such a thing!"

"It's just for a moment." His eyes pleaded. "Billy's here, you see."

"Billy? Who on earth is Billy?"

"Why, he's just the most famous rat dog there is, that's all." Jem poured out his scorn upon her ignorance. "He's been known to kill a hundred rats at a go, 'e has." He waxed enthusiastic while quite failing to take note of his companion's deepening disgust. "And I've placed a monkey on 'im and I just can't miss the chance of seeing Billy in the flesh, now, can I? Come on. There's bound to be some other females there."

Louisa thought this quite improbable and was about to volunteer to wait for him outside when two inebriated young farmers came rolling out of the building, passing their jug convivially back and forth. Catching sight of Louisa, they nudged one another joyfully and leered in her direction. "I say there, lad," they called out to Jem, " 'old on a minute. That's too much woman for the likes of ye."

Sighing, Louisa capitulated. "All right, then. We'll go in. But mind you, just for a minute. Once you've seen the famous Billy, then we leave."

"Oh, I say, you are a sport!" Jem clapped her on the arm hastily and headed for the door. Louisa trailed behind him.

The first thing that struck her was the stench: sweating human bodies crammed together in the airless room, dog excretion, smoking lanterns, and something indefinable that she later recognized as blood.

A plank-lined pit was flanked by a double deck of wooden bleachers crammed with spectators, all male as far as Louisa could see at first until she spied a female or two of the coarse variety that put her to the blush. Her discomfort was not aided by the heads that turned curiously her way to leer and whistle. Fortunately, though, most had their attention riveted on the pit. "Let's go, Jem," she hissed, but it was too late. The little fifteen-year-old was snaking his way through the crowd to get a ringside view. Louisa tried to follow and retrieve him, then made the evening's second terrible mistake. She looked down into the pit.

The surface crawled with rats—hundreds of rats, running helter-skelter for their lives, careering into the wooden barrier, trampling the mangled carcasses of their fellow creatures, while trying to escape the savage, snarling jaws of a small white terrier dotted with black spots who tore viciously just then at one squealing rodent while the crowd cheered him on.

Louisa stood for a moment rigid with horror, then gagged and bolted for the door. If she had remembered the drunken farmers, she would have found them preferable to the loathsome rat pit and the depraved humanity that crowded it.

Outside she took deep, shuddering gulps of the fresh air and hung on to a tree trunk for support.

"I think that keeping one's head down is generally considered a safeguard against a swoon." Lord Lyston spoke behind her with clinical detachment.

"I've never swooned in my life." Louisa managed a shaky sort of indignation.

"I can't tell you how glad I am to hear it. Smelling salts? Burnt feathers? The antidotes for vapors are beyond my ken."

Louisa took a few more gulps of air then turned to face him. He might well have been in the Bath Assembly Rooms, not an open field, for he was dressed in the requisite knee smalls, white hose, and gleaming pumps. In spite of her touch-and-go queasiness, Louisa took due note of his well-shaped legs before raising her eyes to his black coat, snowy cravat, and—finally—the blue eyes that watched her so mockingly.

"Ah, that's better," he remarked, folding his arms across his chest. "You aren't looking nearly so greenish as before. May I say, Mrs. Varley, that you astonish me? Your colorful friend of the Theatre Royal did inform me of your passion for the pit, but the *rat* pit?" His brows shot up, and he shook his head in mock amazement.

"Well, I'm sure you're no more astonished by my presence here than I am by yours. For I can only surmise that you, at least, came of your own volition. And of all the disgusting, loathsome, depraved—"

"I get your drift and won't quarrel with your review," he interrupted. "I saw your young swain—he is the stripling of the dress and sword, is he not? I thought so. I saw him desert you and wondered whether you'd make it outside without a disaster. Now I think I should take you home."

"That won't be necessary." Louisa made herself speak civilly, for though she didn't like his mocking attitude, she knew a rescue when she saw it. The drunken farmers had taken their jug and retreated around the building after he'd sent one quelling glare their way. "I would be grateful, however, if you'd go back in that place"—in spite of herself, she shuddered, and Lord Lyston grinned—"and fetch Jeremiah for me."

"No," he answered curtly. "From the looks of you, you'd never make it home on foot. And I think it will do young Scopes a bit of good to wonder what's become of you." Ignoring her protests, Lyston led her across the field to where a handsome pair of matched grays were harnessed to a high-perch phaeton that caused Louisa's eyes to widen at its elegance. In spite of herself she breathed a heartfelt sigh as she leaned back on the deliciously soft leather cushions.

"I take it you are frazzled." Lord Lyston climbed in beside her and clucked expertly at his team.

"Exhausted," she admitted. "We must have walked for miles. And I was tired to begin with. I really wondered how I'd make it back."

"Glad to be of service." He didn't exactly sound it, but Louisa refused to worry over such a trivial matter. Instead she reveled in the unaccustomed luxury of a truly well-sprung rig and removed her chip-straw bonnet to let the cool night breeze ruffle out her hair. They drove in silence for a while. "Who were you tonight?" his lordship asked abruptly.

"What?" Louisa was startled out of the heady pleasures of soaking up the moonlight, admiring the beauty of the purebred animals, and savoring the joy of being in a high-perch phaeton under the somewhat reluctant protection of a true peer of the realm. In fact, she'd quite forgotten who she was.

"Oh, the theater, you mean." She came down to earth. "I was Juliet."

"It suits you." He stared down his aristocratic nose and appraised her carefully. "I mean that you are right, physically, for the part," he qualified. "Most actresses grow as ancient as Mrs. Siddons before they're deemed competent to play Juliet. But

I imagine you contrive to portray all that youth and innocence quite effortlessly."

"Amazing, isn't it, given my past debauchery," Louisa retorted, stung by his implication.

"Yes, I do find it amazing," he replied evenly. "But I can see that you'd carry off the part. I've always considered Romeo a sap-skulled widgeon, personally, to get in such a taking over a girl he'd barely met, but I can see where you might actually have that sort of effect."

"Since I've no idea whether I've been complimented or insulted—but given our past history, I do suspect the latter—I'll not venture a reply."

"Well, actually, I meant neither. I'm merely stating the obvious—that any adolescent male would be turned to idiocy at the sight of you." Louisa took full note that he emphasized the word "adolescent," but she held her tongue. "And so," his lordship continued, "I have no trouble understanding why Adrian was moved to make such a complete cake of himself."

"Do you not, indeed," Louisa replied dangerously, all pleasure from the phaeton ride now vanished.

"None at all. He was barely free of his leading strings, you know."

"No, that I did not know!" She gave him a level look which he returned, leaving the horses to pick their own way down the lane. "And I think you much mistake the matter. Since you were the one who wished to keep him in those leading strings, I suppose you have no way of knowing that Adrian became a man behind your back." They were at daggers drawn now without a doubt. Well, she had known they'd have to come to it.

"No, I did not know about his twenty-year-old manhood. But I assume you were most instrumental in aiding his arrival at that point."

Louisa was well aware of his not-so-veiled meaning, but she did not choose to set the record straight. She was far too incensed to care for his good opinion. In fact, she rather wished it otherwise. "I certainly hope I never treated him like the child you seem determined to consider him," she answered hotly.

"Then I'll have to disillusion you." The tone was harsh, but for a moment Louisa glimpsed in his eyes the pain of Adrian's loss and regretted her hot temper. This compassion was destroyed, however, by his next statement. "I'm afraid it's precisely his relationship with you that makes me doubt his manhood. For you see, only a complete green'un would have married you. A man would have known to offer a *carte blanche*."

Her palm itched to slap his arrogant face again, but she clasped her hands tightly together and fought her temper for control.

"At least it's obvious that Adrian's brother would never let his heart rule his head. I had a few moments at the Royal to observe you and your Miss Sedgwick together. May I hazard a guess about her?" He gave her a dangerous look, but she continued. "An heiress beyond all doubt."

"No doubt at all. Only let me observe that she stands to benefit more from the alliance than I, since my fortune puts hers quite in the shade."

"Indeed?" Louisa sounded skeptical.

"Indeed. Does that upset your theory?"

"Not at all. Except to make me wonder what the great attraction is."

"That's easy to explain. Birth. Breeding. Similarity of background and interest. We grew up together and can have few surprises for one another."

"How stimulating for you," Louisa murmured as he gave her a set-down look. Then suddenly she giggled. "That's it! I have it! I'll bet a monkey her estate marches with yours and that you stand to increase your holdings. Am I not right?"

"You are," he admitted grudgingly, then grinned in spite of himself at her look of triumph. "Well, I fail to see anything so reprehensible in that, Juliet. I happen to think that 'all for love and the world well lost' is a game for sapskulls."

Her face clouded for a moment, recalling Varley. "You're right, of course," she said.

He looked at her curiously. "I hardly expected you to agree so readily. But while we're on the subject, what makes you think that I'm not in love with Miss Sedgwick? I assure you, I hold her in the highest esteem."

"I never doubted it. That's hardly the same thing."

"I wouldn't know." He shrugged. "But I'll bow to your superior wisdom. You're something of an authority in that area, I presume."

"I'm an actress. I make my living by recognizing emotions and then trying to reproduce them."

"Well, I'm sorry if I failed you as a model for Romeo. I'll try and do better the next time I'm with Miss Sedgwick."

"Then she'll have real cause to be grateful to me, won't she?"

"I would not count on it. I think her opinion of you falls far short of yours for her, if you can believe it. And, by the by, I haven't thanked you yet for compromising me so prettily at the Theatre Royal. I was wrong about your limited ability as an actress. You play a London light-skirt to perfection. Your accent fairly set my teeth on edge."

"Yes, but how do you know which was the pretense?" she asked mischievously. "Perhaps that was my true voice quality and I'm acting now."

"I admit the thought has occurred to me. But in either case you deserve kudos for it. And you'll be delighted to know that I spent a chilly evening after that tête-à-tête with your colorful friend."

Louisa giggled at the memory of his companions' reaction to Aunt Nell Scopes. "I am delighted. For you must admit you had it coming."

"I admit nothing of the sort. But, dear God, where did she find those feathers?"

"In the costume department."

"That explains it. From what role, the Huron Chief? Did your gauze thing also come from there?"

She glared at him. "My gown? Are you trying to tell me I looked freakish too?"

"Oh no," he said hastily, "it was almost becoming. That's what made your dockside voice so incongruous, coming from a Romney portrait as it did." And he grinned at the recollection while Louisa noted how nice the change of expression made him look. It occurred to her that the moonlight, the luxury of the ride, and her weariness might have a totally inappropriate effect.

"Er, speaking of costume," she said, changing the subject, "would you satisfy my curiosity? Do you always wear evening smalls when visiting a rat pit?"

He laughed. "No. In fact, I can't claim to be a habitué of rat pits. While they don't have the same queazy effect on me that they do on you, as a sport I'd rank them somewhere below hog butchering. Actually, I began the evening in the Assembly Rooms. But they seemed flatter than usual, which is bad indeed, so an inebriated friend persuaded me to come out here and see the famous Billy."

"Heavens. Where is your friend?"

"Still inside, I suppose."

"You mean you just drove off and left him?"

"Why not? He can walk home with your friend

Jeremiah. Do him no end of good. He's bound to be cold sober when he gets back to York House."

She giggled and slid down upon the seat until her head rested on the soft leather cushion and her face was turned upward to the moon. The horses were practically ambling now. Lord Lyston seemed in no hurry to get home. "Oh, this is nice!" she blurted before she thought. "It's been so long since—" Louisa stopped short, appalled at what she'd almost said.

"Since you've driven in a phaeton? Did Adrian have one?" Lord Lyston's face was harsh once more as he recalled their adversary roles which they had momentarily set aside.

"Not that I was aware of."

"I'm sure you would have known it. By the by, I was proven wrong when I said you'd find my solicitor more difficult to deal with than myself. I thought him old enough to be impervious to your charms. It seems I was mistaken."

She sat up straight again and glared at him. "Why? Why should he behave other than civilly toward me? I've made no demands on him—or on you."

"So he said. The difference between us is that he thinks you never will."

"While you think?"

"Let's just say that I reserve my judgment. It's early days yet. At any rate, I'm going up to London next week. I shall persuade him to draw up a settlement that I don't think you'll treat quite so cavalierly. I don't like loose ends dangling, Mrs. Varley."

"Loose ends? I've been termed a lot of things, but never a 'loose end' before." Her laugh held no humor. They rode in hostile silence for a bit. "When are you going to London?" she inquired, trying to sound casual.

"Next Wednesday. Why?"

"Just making conversation," Louisa replied, though not quite truthfully.

Trim Street was quiet and deserted when his lordship turned into it. The horses' hooves rang loudly through the silence. The house was completely dark, Louisa noted. If the elder Scopeses had returned from the theater, they were already in their beds.

"I do thank you," Louisa turned toward his lordship and began, but she never got a chance to finish the polite platitude that was forming on her lips. For before she'd gained the slightest clue to what he had in mind, Lyston stopped her words effectively by placing his lips roughly upon hers. He also crushed her hard against his chest.

Her first reaction was astonishment. Her next, by all rights, should have been blazing anger. But instead she was swept away upon a sudden tide of emotion unlike any she'd ever known. It had been ages since she'd been able to endure Varley's caresses. And at no time had they ever affected her in quite this way, a circumstance she made excuses for when she recalled it later on, blaming the emotional exhaustion of her stage performance, the fatigue of the long hike to the rat pit, and the moonlight streaming overhead. Lord Lyston's overpowering presence and decided expertise she dismissed as being entirely beside the point.

Louisa rallied eventually and pushed him away. But if she needed any reminder that she'd been rather slow in doing so, the triumphant gleam in his lordship's eyes drove home the fact. "What was all that in aid of?" She asked the question as calmly as she could considering she was suffering from a rather acute shortage of breath.

"Nothing in particular, I suppose," he answered.

"Except that, as I think I owned up to earlier, there's hardly a man alive who could resist doing so. Besides, I wished to conduct a small experiment."

"I know I should not ask," she replied quietly, "but what experiment?"

"One designed to maintain my perspective. You're the first actress I've had any experience of, you see. And it's easy to forget that you can play any part you choose. That of a lady, for example."

She held her eyes steadily on his face. "But now you are sufficiently reminded?"

He nodded coolly.

"For no lady would have kissed you back that way?"

"You take my meaning."

"Well, then, Lord Lyston, I wish you much joy of your Miss Sedgwick. What you've just told me confirms my first impression. You two are quite deserving of one another."

And before he could frame an answer or come round to hand her down, Louisa had jumped out of the high-perch phaeton and fled inside the house.

Chapter Nine

THE KNOCKING WAS TENTATIVE AT FIRST, THEN LOUDER. Louisa sighed and climbed out of bed to answer. A very anxious-looking Jem shielded his candle from a draft while he held it high and examined her for signs of violence. "Thank God!" he breathed. "Those foxed farmers outside the pit said you'd driven off with some gentry-cove. I didn't know if you'd been snatched—or what."

"No, nothing so sinister. A gentleman who'd seen me at the theater offered me a ride home, that's all," Louisa improvised.

"Well, you might have let me know. I was that sick with worry!" Jem made a quick transition from guilt to injury.

"I'm sorry," Louisa said, thinking it was all a piece with her topsy-turvy evening that she should be the one to apologize. "But I could not go back into that awful place. And the gentleman with me would not."

"Well, 'all's well that end's well,'" the fledgling actor quoted grudgingly. "But I say, Louisa, you won't tell Aunt Nell about any of this, will you?"

"I shouldn't think so."

His face outshone the candle. "Oh I say, that's famous. You really are a good fellow, Louisa."

"Thank you, Jem. Good night."

But now that both his anxieties had been relieved, Jem seemed loath to leave. For he had only just noticed Louisa's deshabille, and the effect on him was devastating. His eyes widened, his chin dropped, and the candle in his hand tilted dangerously, allowing wax to splash and harden on his boots.

"Good night, Jem," Louisa said firmly, recalling Lyston's sneering remarks about her appeal for halflings. "We both need our sleep."

But in her case, at least, all hope for sleep was gone. She tossed and turned, tangling the light counterpane while angry tears stung her eyes as she recalled Lyston's humiliating kiss. The anger was soon replaced, however, by shamed confusion at the memory of her strange reaction. Her cheeks burned hot with the thought of it. First there'd been astonishment. But the shock of surprise had been followed quickly by a totally inappropriate sense of having sailed at last into safe harbor after successfully weathering the storms of the past few years. And then to find he was only playing games with her! A London light-skirt indeed! Louisa recalled Lyston's description of his reaction to her voice when she'd greeted him so mischievously at the Theatre Royal. He had claimed then not to know just which role she belonged in. Was she a light-skirt or a lady? But he'd soon made his casting plain enough.

Why she should care how he chose to view her

was more than she was able to sort out. He was rude, arrogant, not all that handsome—that is, if you forgot about his eyes. And perhaps his physique could not be entirely discounted either. He was very rich, of course, and odiously secure of his position in society. No doubt that was the attraction, Louisa analyzed. For she was far too honest not to admit that she was strongly attracted to him. It was no more than a natural longing to go back home, she finally concluded. No doubt about it. It's what Lyston represented that she was in danger of falling in love with. Not the man himself.

When the following Wednesday dawned with a hint of rain, Louisa was almost persuaded to abandon her enterprise. But by the time she had finished Mrs. Bottoms's bountiful breakfast, the sun was peeping through the clouds and the day promised to be fine. Louisa sighed as she lost her last excuse to postpone an unpleasant duty. She went to her room and changed to riding clothes, then set out toward Ryle's in Monmouth Street, where she could rent a mount.

Ever since she had learned from Lyston that Samuel Webster had not survived the Battle of Waterloo, she had felt encumbered to look up his friends and family and tell them what she knew of the private's last heroic hours. But she had been slow in doing so. Two circumstances had stopped her: the difficulty of reporting Webster's gallantry without revealing her own relationship to Adrian, and the unlikelihood of visiting Graylands without encountering Lyston there. Now that the problem of meeting his lordship had been solved by his trip to London, Louisa counted upon the inspiration of the moment to get her over the other hurdle.

As she rode out of town in the direction of

Claverton, the sun was out full force. It beamed down on Mr. Ralph Allen's Sham Castle glimpsed through the treetops in the distance, giving the vista a decided romantic touch. Louisa smiled to herself, thinking that the eccentric gentleman who had had a cockleshell placed on a hillside merely for effect would have surely found a spiritual home in the world of theater. There was something delightful about foisting off that bit of illusion upon the workaday countryside. Louisa urged her horse into a gallop, suddenly feeling joyously lighthearted in spite of the sadness of her mission.

Louisa had no trouble at all in finding Graylands. The first farmer she called to in a field directed her to the proper lane leading off the highroad that he vowed would take her straight to the gates of the estate. Fortunately, those gates were standing open and unattended. She passed through them quite unchallenged and walked her bay mare sedately down the carriage drive, hoping to call no attention to herself.

At first the road rambled through a heavily wooded area, where Louisa was only able to catch occasional glimpses of massive chimneys breaking through the trees. Then she entered into the landscaped portion of the grounds and stopped a moment to gaze out across a vast octagonal pond at the stone structure that was Graylands. The house was an immense rectangular block with no break in its facade. Its doorway boasted no large pediment, and the marble steps leading up to it were flanked by the plainest of balustrades. It was capped, however, by a hipped roof lit by dormer windows and topped with a cupola that gave it some distinction. But all in all, Louisa concluded after studying it intently for a moment, the Grayson seat might at best be called imposing but never handsome.

Since she wished to avoid the house if at all possible, when the drive rounded a curve and suddenly forked, Louisa took the branch that headed away from it. A short time later, she was rewarded for her judgment when the road she'd chosen led her to the stables.

Judged each with its own kind, Louisa ranked the Grayson stables more impressive than the house, which probably showed where the family placed its values, she concluded. Indeed, the entryway that led to the stables was on a slightly grander scale than the portals she'd passed through to reach the carriage drive. Its two large brick pillars were topped with marble pedestals that in their turn were topped with iron gryphons. Louisa rode between the two fierce guardians, which somehow recalled Lord Lyston to her mind, and proceeded down a yew-lined path, and then into the stables proper.

The young lad busy mucking out a stall looked up in astonishment. "May I see the head groom, please?" Louisa asked him. That seemed as good a place to start as any she could think of.

"Yes'm." The lad tugged at his forelock and disappeared. Louisa dismounted, picked up a handful of hay from the manger he'd deserted, and fed it to her horse while "Mr. Archer! Mr. Archer!" the stableboy whooped outside. In a moment, Louisa was joined by a middle-aged man wearing a heavy workshirt and leather vest with his britches tucked down into well worn riding boots. There was no mistaking the air of authority on the weathered face, but it did not obscure the fact that he was quite as curious as the stableboy. "You wanted to see me, miss?" he asked.

Since she could think of no more subtle opening,

Louisa plunged right in. "Actually, I'm looking for someone—anyone—here who might have been close to Private Samuel Webster."

"Well now, miss, they's plenty here who could lay claim to that. And, for that matter, his mother lives no more'n two miles in that direction."

"I'm sorry," Louisa said, "but I really don't think I'll have time to go on farther. I thought perhaps I could tell someone here what I have to say . . ." She left the sentence dangling.

"Well, as for that, I reckon I could pass on any message to Mrs. Webster, miss. And as for Sammy, well you see, miss, I knew him ever since he was a wee lad, with 'im and his lordship playing right here under the horses' legs—and under my feet, too, when it came to that. Then of course after he got a bit of size on 'im, he came to work here, under me." The man's eyes misted over, and he ran a rough sleeve across his nose. "Yes'm. You could say as how I knew Sammy Webster as well as any and better'n most," he finished gruffly.

While the stable lad rubbed down her horse, Louisa and Mr. Archer walked outside. There she poured out the story of Private Webster's final days of heroism, skirting her own involvement as best she could, merely explaining that her husband and Lieutenant Adrian Grayson had been comrades-in-arms and that they'd all become fast friends. Lieutenant Grayson was often in their home, she went on to say uncomfortably, and so, naturally, Private Webster had come to fetch her to the deathbed. She carefully avoided all mention of anything that took place there, and when Mr. Archer said diffidently, "Begging your pardon, miss, but I didn't catch your name," she replied reluctantly that she was Mrs. Varley. None of these people, she told herself, were likely to see "Mrs. Grayson" on the stage. The last thing she wanted was for them to learn of a marriage that they, like the man they worked for, would deem scandalous.

Still, for reasons she herself did not fully understand, Louisa felt it very necessary that Private Webster's friends and family be told how heroically he had behaved, how he'd snatched his young master out from under the hooves and bayonets, and had carried him to Brussels from Quatre Bras. And how he'd then gone back to die. No matter how Lord Lyston might regard Samuel for his part in Adrian's deathbed marriage, at least his friends would know of the soldier's heroism.

Mr. Archer drew a large handkerchief from his pocket and blew his nose long and lustily. "What you're saying don't come as no surprise, miss," he was finally in enough control to say. "Young Sam Webster was a rare one for tending to his duty. That he was. And he was rare fond of young Master Adrian. Would have given his life for the lad I'm sure, miss."

"And will you tell his mother, then? And any other friends who might wish to know of his last hours?"

"You can rest sure of that, miss. I'll go see Mrs. Webster this very evening. And I'll tell his lordship, too."

This definitely had not been part of Louisa's plan. But she could hardly tell Mr. Archer not to. Nor could she ask him not to say who'd told him. Oh, well, what difference did it make. She mentally shrugged off the rush of dismay that hit her. The important thing was that she'd finally discharged the obligation she'd felt for Private Webster.

"Thank you for riding all the way out here, miss," Mr. Archer said as he helped her mount the bay. She smiled good-bye to him and to the stable lad,

112

then rode once more between the glowering gryph-ons and out onto the carriage drive.

Louisa couldn't resist one more pause to look at Graylands. In fact, she would have liked to have ridden closer for a better view, but hardly deemed it prudent. It was bad enough that her visit would be reported to Lord Lyston without the added infor-mation that she'd been seen gawking at his house.

The sound of galloping hooves from the direction of the entrance to the estate jarred her from her contemplation. Since she had no desire to explain her presence to the unknown rider, she urged her own horse forward from the clearing, then dis-mounted and pulled the bay into a concealing thicket. With luck, and given the rate of speed of the galloping equestrian, she should escape his no-tice.

But luck was on the other side of the under-growth. Louisa heard the horse checked suddenly, then Lord Lyston pushed his way through the thick shrubbery. "Oh, there you are," he said. "I was afraid I'd missed you."

Since he'd come in the opposite direction from the stables, Louisa opened her mouth to ask how he'd known she was there. Instead, she blurted, "I thought you'd gone to London," then could have kicked herself.

"I changed my mind. Since you were so curious about when I was going, I wondered if you might not be planning to take a look at Graylands. Well, are you properly impressed?" He nodded at his stately home, which stood out clearly from this side of the screening foliage.

Louisa itched to tell him that she definitely was not impressed, that when compared to her father's hall in Yorkshire, designed by Robert Adam, Graylands lacked both grace and beauty. What it

113

mostly looked was solid and enduring. "When was it built?" she asked after an awkward pause.

"In 1640," he answered haughtily, sensing her lack of admiration. "Sorry I can't offer you towers or mullioned windows, not even a ghost with clanking chains, but would you like a tour?"

"No, thank you. I must return to Bath."

"You've seen the Dower House, then?" Louisa shook her head. "Well then. It won't do for you to leave without seeing that. It was to have been Adrian's. So, if you're planning to make some claim, you'd best have a realistic idea of what you're shooting for. Not that it will do you any good, of course." His tone and face were bland. He might have been the perfect host.

"Lord Lyston," Louisa began angrily, then checked herself. "Indeed, why not?" She shrugged and mounted her horse quickly before he could dismount and help her. His eyebrows rose at her obvious skill. "Lead on," she said.

They rode in silence back down the avenue in the direction of his lordship's house, then circled wide around it and followed a yew-lined lane that wound its way to a grassy lawn broken here and there by massive shade trees. In the center of this clearing stood a handsome graystone cottage, solidly rectangular like the Hall, but a great deal smaller, with only four chimneys rising from its corners. Its walls were softened by climbing ivy and alive with sparkling windows that on the bottom level reached from floor to ceiling, or so Louisa judged from the exterior view.

"Why, it's charming!" she blurted out before she thought and almost laughed aloud at the look of disgust upon his lordship's face. "Indeed," she added mischievously, "I quite prefer it to the Hall."

"Do you indeed! Actually, there's a damp-rot problem. And it's quite cramped, of course."

Louisa suspected he now regretted the impulse he'd had to show it to her. She took advantage of his mood to needle him still further. "I must say, though, it does seem rather unfair for you to have so much"—she gestured theatrically at the huge edifice towering on the hill—"and, by a mere accident of birth, Adrian so little."

"Does it?" he replied frigidly. "In point of fact, things would not have been as inequitable as they seem. Adrian most likely would have continued living at Graylands even after he'd set up his own household. As you can see, there would have been no fear of overcrowding."

"That is, of course, if he married properly."

"Of course. I don't imagine that he intended bringing you to Graylands, Mrs. Varley, if indeed he thought at all, which, given your heady presence, I'm inclined to doubt. Upon reflection, I think he'd have made a career of the army and stayed abroad. Under the circumstances, he'd have had little choice," his lordship finished bitterly.

"Poor Adrian," Louisa thought as she looked at Lord Lyston rather curiously. "How little he understood his older brother. Adrian really thought he was putting me under this man's protection."

Lord Lyston misunderstood her look. "Of course all this is now academic," he went on, "but under better circumstances Adrian would have had some other choices. He could have helped manage the estate and either lived here," he gestured at the Dower House, "or, as I said, at Graylands. Then, too, you must have passed the rectory as you came in." Indeed, Louisa recalled a handsome house she'd seen only a half mile or so from the entrance to the avenue. "The estate does provide quite a

115

good living, which is vacant just at present. I was waiting to fill it until Adrian's discharge, in case he might consider taking holy orders. Still, I doubt that the life of the church would have suited him." He looked her pointedly up and down.

"Oh, I don't know," Louisa replied thoughtfully. "Of course, I never heard him speak of such a possibility. But in some ways he was admirably suited for it. He was certainly not lacking in compassion."

Lord Lyston did not miss her implication. "Whereas you, of course, would have been the perfect parson's wife," he sneered.

"Who knows," she murmured. "You yourself compared me to Mary Magdalen." She smiled up at him impishly.

"As I said, such speculation is academic." She glimpsed a sudden pain reflected in his eyes before he conquered it quickly. "Do you wish to see more before you leave?" he asked brusquely.

It was an obvious dismissal. "No, thank you," Louisa replied politely.

As they turned their horses and rode away, Louisa glanced back at the charming Dower House with a look that was tinged slightly with regret. Then she gazed again at the imposing mansion dominating the countryside. Suddenly she giggled.

"Yes?" Lord Lyston queried.

Her shoulders began to shake. "Tell me," she said when she'd recovered her voice again, "since you are so convinced that I came to Bath in order to see what I might claim as Adrian's widow, just what would you do if, after your marriage to the Honourable Miss Sedgwick, I were to set up household here—under your very noses, as it were? Would we not make a charming ménage of relatives?" And again she went off into a choking bout of laughter at the unthinkable absurdity.

"Forgive me for not sharing your amusement, Mrs. Varley," his lordship said haughtily. "I won't even bother to entertain the possibility. For I can assure you, it will never happen."

"No need to look so Friday-faced. I was merely funning."

"Were you, Mrs. Varley?" Lord Lyston stared stonily ahead. "I rather doubt it, but I do hope so. For both our sakes, not just my own."

"You are all heart, sir," Louisa murmured sarcastically.

Chapter
Ten

WHEN MRS. BOTTOMS TAPPED ON THE DOOR A FEW days later and announced, "There's a gentleman to see you, Mrs. Grayson," Louisa rather expected to find Lord Lyston waiting in the small withdrawing room. She recalled with satisfaction their last encounter when she had definitely bested him. Indeed, as he rode from the Dower House to the main gate with her, he was hard put to hide the fact that he'd made a tactical error in showing her the house while almost daring her to try and claim it. And the mischief alive in her plus a desire to exact revenge for his disturbing kiss had prompted Louisa to do all within her power to fan his lordship's apprehension. Since he was determined to think her a fortune hunter, then she'd play the part. During the remainder of their brief ride together, she had dropped little innocent remarks about the balm of country life after the pressure of the theater and how pleased she'd been to discover how surprisingly short the ride from Bath was.

Lyston had shot her a suspicious look, but had held his temper and tongue in check with a herculean effort that almost sent Louisa off into giggling fits once more. At the gateway he had bidden her the stiffest of good-days and had then galloped back down his driveway in what Louisa thought must be "high dudgeon," though she'd only read the term in books.

And she had not the slightest doubt that he'd then gone haring off directly on his postponed trip to London. She now expected to be confronted with some sort of settlement papers drawn up in his solicitor's office and hand-carried either by Mr. Spenser or Lyston himself. But when she entered the withdrawing room she found, rather to her disappointment, that the waiting gentleman was a stranger.

Well, not quite a stranger. As the man stood up to greet her, Louisa recalled that she had seen him more than once among her audience.

"Allow me to present myself," he said. "I am Samuel Arnold, manager of the Drury Lane Theatre in London, and I'm here to offer you a position there."

He pulled a chair out for her none too quickly, and Louisa collapsed upon it in a daze. She stared wide-eyed and uncomprehending while Mr. Arnold, who controlled one of the two most prestigious theaters in the nation, took full note of her bewilderment and explained at length that he had been searching the provinces for a leading lady to play opposite Drury Lane's new meteoric star, the renowned Edmund Kean.

Louisa had heard of Mr. Kean. The actor had burst upon the London scene a little over a year before, playing Shylock to the delight of the audience and the amazement of the critics, one of whom had written: "Mr. Kean's appearance was the first gleam of genius breaking athwart the gloom of the stage." Already Kean posed a serious threat to the aging Kemble's position as premier actor of the day. And his naturalistic style of acting threatened to overset all the artificial posturing of the past. To hitch her own career to Kean's rising star was a glorious opportunity. Still, Louisa hesitated.

"Really, Mr. Arnold," she protested, "while your offer is most flattering, the fact remains that I lack experience. Mr. Kean played the provinces for years before he tackled London."

"That's quite true," Mr. Arnold answered, "but how better to learn your craft than by apprenticing to a master? Besides," he added candidly, "it's your physical appearance that has convinced me that you are just what is needed opposite Edmund Kean."

Here Louisa wryly recalled Lord Lyston's initial assessment of her ability. "The audience recognized an extraordinarily pretty woman. That is all," he had said after first seeing her on the stage in Bath. "Her performance would have been laughed right out of Drury Lane."

Mr. Arnold rightly interpreted her expression. "Please don't misunderstand me. You are very talented, of course. If I did not think so, I'd not be here. And I'm confident you can soon learn any techniques you have not yet had the time to master. If I spoke of your physical attributes before all else, it's because you would be the perfect foil for Kean. He is quite dark, you know, almost Romany in appearance. Your own fairness would stand out in dramatic contrast. Imagine your Desdemona to his Othello. What visual artistry!"

120

Still Louisa hesitated. She was not sure why. She had thought herself ambitious. And no coward, certainly. She did not think she feared the challenge of the London stage. She did feel a great reluctance to leave the Scopeses. She was most grateful for their taking her on in Brussels when she was destitute. And she knew that without her they'd not fare half so well as they were doing now. But deeper than any gratitude, she felt real affection for the manager and for his son and for his eccentric aunt. But whether the Scopes family was her true reason for wishing to remain in Bath, she herself honestly did not know.

When she tried to explain to Mr. Arnold about her obligation to the company, the London manager answered solemnly, "Your loyalty does you credit, m'dear, but you can't afford to let it be a millstone around your neck—as I'm sure Mr. Scopes himself will be the first to tell you. Change is the order of the day, and actors don't dare ignore the knock of opportunity. It might not be so obliging the second time, you know. But I realize all this has been very sudden, m'dear. So let me give you a few days to think the matter over; then we'll talk again. In the meantime I'll speak to the Drury Lane committee. Then we'll be able to discuss actual contract terms as well as other bits of business you'll be wanting to think about." And, with a courtly bow, he left her.

Louisa was much too agitated by the Mr. Arnold's visit to settle down to needlework or reading or any other of those recreations she employed when not performing. What she needed most was solitude and time to think. So, pausing only long enough to tie the ribbons of a cambric muslin bonnet in a becoming bow underneath her chin, she set out to walk the few blocks that led to the towers and terraces of Bath Abbey on the River Avon.

Louisa had thought that sitting in the abbey sanctuary might calm her racing mind. But after a while she found that she could bear to sit no longer. The sunshine, making rainbow patterns through stained glass, seemed to beckon her out of doors. She decided to walk off her agitation down by the river bank.

The route she chose led her past the Pump Room, a choice she regretted instantly when Lord Lyston came striding out the door. "There you are!" he snapped, as though she were a genie he'd rubbed a lamp for. "I need to talk to you."

Even if his aspect had not been so forbidding, Louisa had far too much on her mind just then for one of their famous set-tos. "I'm sorry, Lord Lyston," she replied in a tone fully as imperious as his own. "I fear I haven't the time just now. Another day, perhaps."

"Nonsense. I've wasted enough time already looking for you. Don't you ever tell the people you live with what you're up to? When I went to Trim Street, that toothless horror of an actress thought you'd gone off to the library. I've been to every circulating library in Bath and just now wasted my time looking over the crowd in there." He jerked his head back toward the Pump Room.

"You should have tried the pastry shop. I'm quite addicted to Bath buns, and at least you would have picked up sustenance."

"I'm really not in the mood for your sense of humor, Mrs. Varley," Lord Lyston snarled.

"And I'm not in the mood to be harangued, so if you'll excuse me."

"Well, I won't. I damn well mean to talk to you. I can do it right here with all these mineral-water drinkers stumbling over us to get in and out to that cursed fountain, or we can go somewhere and sit down in peace. What is your pleasure?"

"My pleasure is to be left alone. But since you obviously have no intention of doing so, I had planned to walk down by the river. You may come along," she said grudgingly. "Though what I can have done to put you in such a taking I've no idea. Indeed, on second thought, I question the wisdom of my choice of walks. In your present mood, I would not put it past you to heave me into the river."

"Don't tempt me, Mrs. Varley," he said nastily, and they trudged in silence for a bit until they were free of other strollers.

"Well?" Louisa looked up inquiringly.

"We have been in each other's company alone, how many times now?" Lyston snapped. "Three or four at least."

"I'm sorry. I fear I have not kept score."

"Don't be flippant. The point is, why did you not tell me what you apparently rode all the way out to Graylands to tell my servants?"

"I beg your pardon. I was under the distinct impression—gleaned from you, of course—that I rode to Graylands in order to covet it."

"Stop it!" He wheeled on her furiously, white with anger and something else. "Did it never occur to you that I might care to hear of my brother's last few hours—and Sam Webster's, who was like another brother?"

"Why should it occur to me?" Louisa replied as calmly as she could. "You seemed to be quite well informed on Adrian's final hours. By Lady Follett, I assume. And I never suspected that you'd care to hear my version, or give any credit to it for that matter."

"You could have told me how Sammy rescued

Adrian." He choked and stopped while Louisa looked at him in alarm, wondering whether the steely Lord Lyston was actually going to break down in front of her. But then he quickly channeled his grief back into anger. Perhaps that's what he's been doing all along, she thought as he glared at her with a stony expression that did not entirely mask his pain.

"I realize I should have told you," Louisa answered more reasonably than she might have done a bit before. "In fact, when you brought me home from the rat pit the other night, I did consider it. But then you terminated all conversation, you may recall."

"A likely story."

"But true." So much for pity. Her hackles were up again. "I did want to tell you how terribly concerned Private Webster was that you'd think he failed you—in not looking out properly for Adrian, I mean. And he wanted you to know he'd done his best. It was impossible—"

"You bitch!" Lyston was white and shaken. His eyes burned into hers. She recoiled as though he'd struck her.

"How dare you speak to me like that!" Tears sprang into her eyes and humiliated her even further.

"Why don't you just go on and say what you are thinking?" he replied savagely. "God knows I've said it to myself. I killed the both of them."

She stared at him, appalled, all her own hurt evaporating before his larger suffering. "But that's ridiculous!" she blurted out. "You did no such thing."

"Of course I did. I knew I never should have bought Adrian that damned commission. It was nothing but weakness that made me finally give in to him."

"Fustian. No one who has been in your company for five minutes could possibly accuse you of being weak. You simply recognized the fact—and I must say it took you long enough—that you could not live Adrian's life for him, that's all." She spoke quite matter-of-factly, but there was a tinge of "governess to recalcitrant child" about her tone that Lyston seemed to recognize.

He laughed harshly. "You do have a way of pouring cold water on a fellow, haven't you?"

"Self-pity doesn't much become you. All in all, I rather prefer your 'lord of the manor' arrogance. You seem typecast for it. Besides, you're talking nonsense."

"Well," he rallied, "so much for Brother Adrian. Granted, perhaps, the choice was his. But you can't wipe out my responsibility for Sammy quite so easily. He seems to have told you that I sent him along with Adrian."

"That's true. Of course, I was around Samuel Webster only a little while. And did I say that I admired him tremendously?" Her eyes misted over then and earned her a look from his lordship that was almost approving. "But anyhow," she went on, "I think you gain true understanding of people in times of stress. And I know that Private Webster was his own man, quite as much as you. I don't think you or anyone else could have ordered him to do anything he did not choose to—no matter how many generations the Websters may have been the Grayson servants. He still didn't strike me as a forelock puller. I hope that doesn't disappoint you."

"My God, you do play rough, don't you!" Lyston glared at her. But Louisa noted that he was rapidly becoming his old self again. "You don't mind jumping on a man's rawer feelings in hobnailed boots, now, do you?"

"Not if it seems necessary. In spite of what you believe about me, I'm not really as old as you are, Lord Lyston." Louisa sounded rather miffed and he suddenly lost his tenseness and laughed genuinely. "But even if I have not lived as long, I've learned one thing that you must have missed so far. I know there's nothing so destructive as self-pity. And nothing is a worse waste of time."

"Thank you, madam. I'll try and remember your little homily." He made a mocking bow.

"See that you do." She turned them back in the direction they had come from. "You ought also to recall that Private Webster wasn't killed while looking after Adrian." And she went on to tell him about the private's sense of urgency to get back to his outfit in time for Waterloo.

There were tears in Lyston's eyes then that he didn't try to hide. "I should have gone, too," he said. "I think that's one reason I feel so guilty. From the very first I wanted to join Wellington on the Peninsula. And if my father had lived, I should have done so. But by then I was Lyston of Graylands and had a duty here," he finished bitterly.

"Surprisingly enough," Louisa said airly, "the British Army managed to get the job done anyway."

"Damn you." He laughed wryly. At this point they were almost back to the Pump Room again. "You were dead right about one thing. You *do* stand in some danger of being thrown into the river. Pity it's too far a toss from here."

But Louisa was not listening. She was staring past his shoulder with a stricken expression upon her face, which had suddenly gone white. Lyston turned quickly and looked in the direction of her gaze. But the only thing to be seen was a knot of dowagers gossiping near the entrance to the Pump Room and an elderly gentleman being helped from a sedan chair while roundly scolding a servant who was a bit too slow in handing him his cane.

"For God's sake, what's the matter? You look as though you might have seen a ghost."

"I think perhaps I have." Louisa barely managed to choke out the words. "Now, if you'll excuse me." And without waiting for his reply, she turned and walked away rapidly in quite the opposite direction of the house in Trim Street.

Chapter Eleven

IN A LIFE PLAGUED WITH DIFFICULTIES, ONE OF THE most difficult things Louisa had ever had to do was to sit down and tell the Scopeses of her decision to leave their company.

Mr. Scopes had tried to make it easier. "Well, to tell you the truth, Louisa, this ain't the surprise to us you thought it might be. We've been in this business far too long not to know Arnold of the Drury Lane when we see him. Aunt Nell spotted him in the audience right away, didn't you, Auntie?"

Aunt Nell nodded knowingly. "And though we did think for a while there as it was me he'd come down to see, we finally concluded he could of been interested a bit more in you." The old lady snorted at her witticism.

"But what will you do if I leave right away?"

"What we've always done. Find somebody else. We've been talking the matter over, and though Betty's a right green'un"—Betty was the ingenue

128

they'd just picked up, a runaway from Bristol—"she's got some promise."

"I'd like to say I could stay until she's had more training, but—"

"Say no more," Mr. Scopes interposed. "You don't have to explain. It's what any one of us here would do if we was in your place and got the chance. It's what this business is all about. Lord, child, there's not a player on any circuit in any province what wouldn't give his right arm to play London. No need to feel bad about advancing yourself. That's the whole idea of this or any other profession worth being in."

"But it isn't that. My reasons for leaving are personal, not professional. Actually, I told Mr. Arnold I'd have to think about it, that I wasn't sure I was ready yet."

"As for being ready," Aunt Nell said, "you're ready when you get the chance, for that's the only thing that counts. Lord, look at me! I've been ready these fifty years, and nothing come of it. And as for your personal reasons, I'll eat my last purple turban if you ain't running away from that Lord Lyston. And a right good job of work I'd call it, too. Not that I can blame you if you was to lose your head. God knows, if I was your age and he cut those eyes at me, I'd throw my cap over the windmill quicker than he could blink. But then I always was a fool where the men were concerned. And I'm here to say no good ever come of it. No, ma'am. The best way to get along in this world is to learn to rely on yourself. Those gentry-coves will promise the moon with a ribbon on it, but then let an actress take on a few extra pounds or come down with a terminal case of wrinkles, and it's 'thank ye kindly' and on to the next. And if you don't believe me, you can just ask Mary Robinson or some other of the fat Regent's castoffs."

Louisa opened her mouth to deny that she was running away from Lyston, then closed it without speaking. After all, that did make an acceptable excuse. And she could hardly tell the Scopeses that she was leaving because she'd seen her father in front of the Pump Room that afternoon and knew for certain she could no longer stay in Bath.

Lord Faircot had doubtlessly come again to take the cure and would stay for several weeks, if indeed he had not decided to reside permanently at the health spa. And though there was little danger of his coming to their theater, his servants might. Most of them were sure to have been with him for donkey's years and would recognize Louisa immediately. No, she could not go skulking around Bath corners, always afraid at any moment of running into someone from her past life. It was unthinkable. London now seemed the only logical course to take. And if the Scopeses chose to think that she was in full flight from Lord Lyston, well, perhaps there was a grain of truth in that as well.

The parting was a painful one on Louisa's side and hard, she thought, for the Scopeses as well. Even Mrs. Bottoms was visibly upset. Actress or no, Louisa had brought a touch of gentility to her house. The landlady had been quite impressed by her class of visitors. Besides, there was now a room to let. Mrs. Bottoms was a bit consoled, however, to learn that Louisa's successor at the theater would also take her place at Trim Street. Still, any replacement the Scopeses might find was likely to be only a common actress.

Jem carried Louisa's baggage to the White Horse for her, where she boarded the public coach for London. He stood and waved glumly and she waved back until the vehicle turned a corner and blotted him from view.

As the coach rattled its way past York House, heading toward the London Road, Louisa shrank back against the cushions in case her father might be staying there. More than likely he was back at the Royal Crescent, though, she thought. Lord Faircot was a man who resisted change of any kind.

When the horses left the town behind and toiled uphill, Louisa turned for a long, last look at Bath nestled snugly down below. She tried to imprint the view upon her memory as though it were an artist's painting. The Abbey dominated the landscape; then scattered church spires and chimney pots drew the eye across it. White stone buildings furnished highlights. "I was happy there," Louisa thought with some surprise, remembering first the satisfaction that had come with her small theatrical success and then recalling the Scopes family with affection. "And I've made some good friends, too, that I'm sorry to leave behind." What a pity that her own father—yes, and Lord Lyston, too—could not be considered in their number.

The moment she was ushered into Mr. Arnold's office at Drury Lane, Louisa knew that she had made a tactical mistake. The manager was very glad to see her—that was not the problem, though Louisa had been plagued by doubts during the coach ride that he might have changed his mind and hired some other actress to play opposite Edmund Kean. But no, Mr. Arnold still desired her, that he made quite clear. Louisa recognized to her regret, however, that the manager was well aware that she had burnt her bridges now and he'd have no need to pay her a decent wage. And she kicked herself for being panicked into leaving Bath so soon. If she had held her ground and made him come to her, she might have had some leverage to bargain.

As it was, when Mr. Arnold offered her a mere five pounds a week and she protested, Louisa knew it was a waste of breath. And when the smiling Arnold pointed out her lack of experience in a major company, he did not refrain from mentioning that he was parroting her own words. "But only five pounds at Drury Lane!" Louisa sounded shocked. The manager shrugged apologetically and went on to speak of the hard times that the theater had been facing. "Why, Kean himself had to start with six." Mr. Arnold had played his high card, and Louisa sighed in capitulation. There seemed to be no hope for her but poverty if the company's leading tragedian had had to be content at first with only one pound more.

As the interview progressed, though, Louisa soon suspected that money might not be the worst of her problems there at Drury Lane. There was something in the manager's tone when he spoke of Edmund Kean that caused her thumbs to start to prick. Every bit of high-flown praise the manager bestowed upon the actor, who was bringing the audiences once more to Drury Lane and causing Covent Garden severe anxiety, seemed to be followed by a qualifier that boded no good for her new relationship. For example, "dramatic genius" was clearly allied to "aristic temperament," and "magical audience appeal" was followed by "inclined to be a bit difficult with his colleagues."

Well, that problem would have to wait for later. At least she had considerable experience with difficult men, Louisa thought wryly as Mr. Arnold ushered her from his office and offered a few words of advice about where she might look for lodgings.

The advice was good and no doubt kindly meant, but Louisa soon discovered she could not afford to follow it.

After hours of trudging about and knocking upon doors and lowering her requirements to fit her purse, Louisa finally found a room in Cecil Street near the Strand. It was cramped and none too clean, and the memory of Mrs. Bottoms's pleasant airy bedchamber almost brought the tears. But this was the best she'd seen that she could afford; reluctantly she parted with the rent demanded in advance.

"It's not that I don't trust ye, dearie," the crone who owned the house informed her. "It's just that I 'appen to know from 'ard experience that actors soon get parted from their brass, and it's best to take it while it's there."

No doubt she was right, Louisa decided as she unpacked her things and tried to rid the tiny room of the worst of its accumulated grime. Her money was certainly dwindling fast, and she felt a sudden surge of panic at being all alone. Louisa gave herself a mental shake. As Aunt Nell said, how many actresses out there in the provinces wouldn't give their right arms to be in her place right now. Leading Lady of Drury Lane! What a pity, she mused glumly, that there wasn't a good hot meal to go with all the glory.

The next few weeks were to teach Louisa just how well the Scopeses had sheltered her from the more sordid aspects of a theatrical career. She had not been entirely blind, of course, to the low esteem in which actors were generally held, but she had been inclined to write the attitude off as snobbery. Now she was rapidly learning that all too many members of her new profession justified the unsavory reputation that tainted it.

For example, it did not take her long to discover that her new address was little more than a house of ill repute. Most of the "actresses" who lived there only occasionally appeared upon the stage. They earned their living, in the main, through practicing an older, more dubious profession. Louisa did her best to avoid this type and quickly earned a reputation for snobbery and the name "Her Ladyship" that she often heard whispered behind her back. "Living here is only temporary," Louisa tried to reassure herself. "When I know London better, I'll find another place. For now, this is cheap, at least. And close to Drury Lane."

All her hopes now focused upon her career. There seemed no other future for her. She was cut adrift, carried farther and farther from everything she'd known. For the first time, she was entirely on her own.

For even after her father had disowned her, there still had been the regiment: a tight social world in which an officer's wife had automatic status. And Bath's familiarity had protected her old identity. Now in London, Louisa hardly knew herself and was beset with doubts about her future. Only her pride, stiffened by the vision of a possible encounter with her father, prevented her from fleeing back to Trim Street. For she could not bear to have Lord Faircot discover that his worst predictions about her future had been justified. Let him think she was still married and on the Continent. Since he'd forbidden her name ever to be spoken in his presence, he was unlikely to learn otherwise. Unless the two of them should meet. And she would not risk that. Besides, there was another danger in a return to Bath that she also knew she must avoid. And so she gritted her teeth and pinned her hopes on Drury Lane.

But even that faint hope gradually gave way to apprehension. The new season was set to open in October. For weeks the company had been going through the motions of rehearsal without their star. Now, as opening night drew near, the great Kean had still not arrived. He was making a fortune, so his envious and unadmiring colleagues said, by playing Ireland and the provinces and had no qualms at all about overstaying his allotted time. Kean, it appeared, was a law unto himself.

Louisa was hearing more and more unsavory stories about the actor. He had arrived at Drury Lane the year before, worn down and shabby, begging for a chance, and had been an instantaneous, electrifying hit. He had saved the theater from bankruptcy and closure. Now his arrogance knew no bounds. There might be a committee and a manager who nominally ran the theater, but it was Edmund Kean who really called the tunes.

"And 'e's jealous as all 'ell," a fellow actor told Louisa for about the dozenth time. She no longer wondered why she, an unknown, had stepped into the exalted position of leading actress. Everyone in the entire company had either implied the reason or had bluntly voiced it. No one could play with Kean. He had driven established actresses to tears right on the stage. And woe betide the leading lady who got some share of the audience acclaim. She soon found herself unemployed. The same held true of supporting players of either sex. A Kean performance was a one-man show.

The stories of Kean's tyranny over his fellow players were certainly disturbing to a young woman who wished to carve out a lasting theatrical career. But Louisa found Kean's acting reputation more tolerable than the unsavory character he enjoyed offstage. Even in a profession hardly known for its puritanism, the star's debauchery was scandalous. It was the talk of the theatrical community, and in spite of all the efforts of the Drury Lane Committee to hush it up, Kean's depravity was also fast becoming public knowledge. Indeed, those closest to the genius were wondering if he was not perhaps a little mad. Certainly Kean was driven by demons well beyond even his own understanding or power to control.

All in all, Louisa approached her opening night in London with a mounting dread. Dread increased to panic on the day of her debut when she arrived at the theater for the last rehearsal and Edmund Kean still had failed to come.

They were to open in *Othello*, a role that many critics considered to be Kean's greatest triumph. Hazlitt had called his performance "the finest piece of acting in the world," and had further written that Kean bore on his brow "the mark of the fire from Heaven." Louisa had been cast as Desdemona, a taxing role in the best of circumstances and one that daunted actresses far more seasoned and renowned than she. Now it appeared that if, in fact, the play went on, which seemed more and more unlikely, she would have to play her part without benefit of any rehearsal with the star.

"Never mind, m'dear." After the sham dress rehearsal wound down to a dismal close, Mr. Pope, who played Iago, tried to reassure her. "Kean most likely will show up. Even he daren't push the committee over the brink by not appearing after the playbills have been circulating for weeks. Relax. Don't worry so much about your part. Remember, all you're expected to do is feed Kean his cues. He'll do the rest. Believe me. He always does."

Chapter
Twelve

*L*OUISA'S PANIC WAS NOT ALLAYED BY MR. POPE'S RE-
assurance, nor by the throngs gathered at the
box office hours before it was due to open. The sus-
pense of whether or not the star would actually
appear—for word of his French leave had spread
throughout the city—seemed only to add to the
frenzy that an appearance by Edmund Kean always generated. Wagers were being laid, and the
bets against Kean's showing up were running high.
In the past, Kean's failures to appear had been explained away as "illness" or "accident." But the
public was no longer quite so gullible. The word
was spreading that Kean was "in his cups."

This time those betting against Kean were
doomed to lose their blunt, though their hopes ran
high till nearly curtain time. Louisa was costumed
and applying makeup with a hand deplorably inclined to shake when she heard a resonant male
voice declaim, "Where is this Mrs. Grayson that the

playbill calls my Desdemona?" The door of her dressing room burst open, and Kean appeared, followed closely by Mr. Arnold.

The star, too, was in costume and made up for the part he'd play, and Louisa's first impression was typical of countless others in her field: "He's small." That fact hit her with a shock. Even though she'd heard it mentioned numerous times before, still she was surprised. Tragic actors tended to be tall—take Mr. Kemble, for example. Besides, Kean's reputation was more than giant-sized.

Louisa's second impression quickly brushed aside the first but was not more original: "He's not dark enough." For Kean had created quite a stir by departing from tradition. He refused to play the Moor with a jet-black complexion and had adopted brown greasepaint in order that his expressions might be better seen.

In the short time that Louisa had been gaping at Edmund Kean, the famous coal-black stare had been assessing her. "It says here"—he waved the playbill he was clutching in his hand—"that you are Mrs. Grayson 'this being her first appearance at Drury Lane.' Well, my dear, is this also your first appearance anywhere?"

"No," Louisa managed to choke out, then added, "Of course not" with a bit more assertiveness.

"That is a relief. You look young enough to have come straight from the schoolroom. Where?"

"I beg your pardon?"

"Where have you played?" He might have addressed the village idiot.

"In Bath," she answered coldly, taking an intense dislike to the little man.

"Oh, yes, Bath. I, too, have played there."

Louisa did not correct his false impression that it was the Theatre Royal she alluded to. She knew she would need all the status she could get to weather Mr. Kean.

"They said you were a beauty, and you are." Kean hardly seemed pleased by the confirmation. "Stand up," he said.

Louisa almost refused to do so, then realized how childish that would be. She stood. Edmund Kean's features distorted into rage. "He was right about the makeup," Louisa thought distractedly. "It certainly doesn't hide emotion."

"It won't do!" Kean turned to Arnold in a fury. "She's too tall entirely. You must have realized it!"

"B-but she's not as t-tall as you are."

Louisa doubted that was true. At least the eyes that were glaring in her direction seemed upon a level with her own. She stared right back, and Kean finally turned away abruptly. "Well, there's nothing to be done about it now." His emphasis on the "now" should have chilled Louisa's blood. It would certainly have had that desired effect upon most audiences. But Louisa perversely was feeling calm again. Suddenly she did not care—about what Kean thought of her or about the good opinion of the audience. She was an actress with a part to play. She would try and bring Desdemona to life upon the stage to the best of her ability. That was all she could do. And if it wasn't good enough, the world would keep on turning.

Later, what she was to remember most about the night was the sheer power of Kean's performance. His genius had not been exaggerated. He portrayed the nobility, the manliness, the tenderness of Othello in a way that Louisa felt only Shakespeare himself could have conceived. She was dazzled by his performance and swept up by it. And upon one level of her mind she was conscious of transcending her own previous pedestrian attempts at acting, being pulled up by the bootstraps as it were by Kean's inspired portrayal of the Moor, striving to make her Desdemona worthy of all that fire and passion. And that self beyond her self was also conscious of the fact that she alone of all the cast was playing up to Kean. The rest were merely following Pope's advice and feeding the star his lines.

But as Desdemona's death approached, Louisa shed her character and began to feel real fear. For she wondered if Kean himself along with the part he played had passed the bounds of sanity. "Thank God I'm to be killed behind the closed curtains of the bed," she thought. If Kean had been directed to smother her with the audience looking on, Louisa had little doubt but that he would do it thoroughly. When the bed hangings opened and she lay there stage-corpse still, she raised a thankful prayer that she was indeed alive. Then she began to concentrate so hard on not letting out a "whoof" as Othello stabbed himself and his body plummeted upon hers that she was quite unprepared for the final curtain or for the thunderous applause that followed it. Amid all the shouts of "Kean! Kean! Kean!" she almost thought she heard faint echoes of "Mrs. Grayson!" But the malignant glance the star shot at her as he swept offstage destroyed any triumph she might otherwise have felt.

The next day the *Morning Chronicle* carried a glowing account of the Great Man's return to Drury Lane. The critic marveled that Kean's *Othello* continued to reach new heights of raw emotion. "And for the first time," the writer went on to add, "Drury Lane has found a Desdemona worthy of Othello's transports of passion. Mrs. Grayson's delicate, fair beauty was the perfect foil for the swarthy Moor, and the bewildered pathos that she brought to the part of the poor doomed creature made the tragedy of the maddened Moor too horrifying for mere words to convey."

Louisa clipped the piece, intending to send it to the Scopeses. But she read it over and over again first, reveling in the bit that dealt with her in spite of the fact that any digression from Kean's glory seemed almost beside the point as far as the thrust of the article was concerned.

Her little triumph was short-lived, though. That afternoon she answered a knock upon her door and was quite surprised to find Mr. Arnold standing there with a copy of the *Chronicle* in his hand, which he presented to her with a courtly bow.

While he occupied the bedroom's only chair, Louisa sat upon the side of the bed and eyed him apprehensively. Mr. Arnold was a manager, not an actor, and had not mastered the art of masking his emotions. Louisa knew that something was very wrong.

He began by congratulating her upon her performance and saying that he heartily agreed with everything the *Chronicle* reviewer had said about her. "In fact, Mrs. Grayson, he quite understated the impact of your performance on the audience."

"Thank you," Louisa murmured, waiting for what followed.

"But I'm afraid, my dear, there is a problem. To put it bluntly, Mr. Kean refuses to appear again with you as Desdemona. So, under the circumstances I'm afraid I have no choice." He bogged down under the gravity of what he had to say.

"You mean that I'm discharged?" Louisa's words were barely whispered.

"No—no—it's not so bad as that," the manager went on hastily. "I told Mr. Kean that you have a contract, that you'd left a good position—no, no, we'll not do that. It's just that—well, you do know

I tried to warn you of Kean's temperament. He cannot share the stage. The other players have come to recognize that fact and have adapted to it. Just as you will in time, m'dear. But for now—I have persuaded him to let you appear again, only no longer as the lead, you understand. He wants a more mature actress in that part. But I've told him you've played Emilia before—that is so, is it not?" Louisa nodded dumbly. "Well, now," Mr. Arnold said a bit too heartily, "that's that then." He rose to his feet. "Thursday you'll play Emilia—at the same salary, naturally." He headed for the door in obvious relief that he'd have no fit of the vapors from her to cope with after having barely survived a stormy scene with Kean. "Oh my dear." He paused with his hand upon the doorknob. "There is just one more thing."

"Yes?" Louisa asked him dully.

"Take my advice, will you, m'dear, and don't play Emilia very well." He closed the door softly behind him and hurried down the stairs.

Louisa did, in time, appreciate the fact that the manager of Drury Lane was doing all within his power to see to it that she kept her job. On performance night he sent in an expert to do her makeup, with strict orders that she was to draw no more attention away from Mr. Kean by reason of her striking looks. Mr. Arnold himself checked the results before curtain time and seemed confident that Louisa was sufficiently unattractive and unrecognizable to placate the jealous star.

Louisa was content to hide behind her makeup. She craved anonymity, or thought she did until the announcement that Miss Ford would play Desdemona's part was followed by a chorus of boos and hisses from the audience. Then, for a moment, she felt a rush of gratitude for those patrons who had either seen her performance on Monday night or

142

had read the *Chronicle* review. Common sense soon told her, though, that the reaction was probably more anti-Kean than pro–Mrs. Grayson. For despite Kean's acknowledged brilliance on the stage, the public was beginning to disapprove of his libertine behavior off the boards and to resent his cavalier treatment of his fellow actors. But whatever the motive, Louisa realized after her initial pleased reaction that the audience protest would not make her position any easier. As much as she longed to see the last of Drury Lane, she had nowhere else to go. And her tenure there depended upon her not antagonizing Edmund Kean.

The play went well enough, though Louisa thought that Kean failed to reach the artistic heights of his previous performance and took malicious pleasure in the fact that the star did himself disservice by not allowing his cast to play up to him.

She acted her own part with complete detachment, giving just enough not to make the character ludicrous. But all the while she was carefully underplaying, Louisa took pains to study every nuance of the Kean technique and file it away in her mind to be pulled out and perfected at a later date.

The Monday-night performance had been time suspended, over before she knew it; this one lasted an eternity. With relief, Louisa watched the curtain finally descend.

The Great Man swept past Louisa without a glance, hurrying to the dressing room where his public was already beginning to collect. Kean had garnered quite a following among the *ton*, including that other famous lion of the day, Lord Byron, who seemed to enjoy the unusual role of playing court after all the adulation he'd received.

Louisa was much too weary to pay attention to

143

that gathering as she passed by Kean's open door on her way to the supporting players' dressing room beneath the stage. She supposed them to be the same fawning group who had gathered around the star before the play to watch him apply the famous makeup.

"Well, I have spent all evening wondering if that drab on the stage could possibly be you."

"Lord Lyston! What on earth are you doing here?" Louisa gasped.

"If you mean in London, I live here—a good portion of the year, at least. If you mean at Drury Lane, I happen to be with a group of stage-struck imbeciles." He nodded with disgust toward Kean's sycophants.

She intended then to walk on past him, but he strolled along. "I'd much rather watch you dress than Kean," his lordship drawled. He looked very distinguished, yes, and handsome, too, Louisa thought, in his severe black-and-white evening clothes. She could not recollect just why at first she had not thought him in the least good-looking. Lyston, however, did not seem nearly so in charity with her appearance. He was looking her critically up and down. "As I was saying, I'll come and watch you dress. Frankly, I'm curious to see if you can possibly be restored to anything near your former beauty. I've heard of hiding a light underneath a bushel, but this is ridiculous."

He strolled into the dressing room with an easy familiarity that made Louisa suspect that this was not a first visit there for him. Nor, indeed, was he the only member of the *ton* in that assembly. The actresses of the company had almost as large a following as Edmund Kean. Louisa and Lord Lyston were the targets of whispering, nudging, and know-

144

ing glances as her fellow players leaped to obvious conclusions.

"Thank God," Lyston said when she'd removed her wig and the disguising putty. "I never actually thought to see you so restored. Only"—he squinted at her quizzically in the glass—"did you not look healthier in Bath? I could swear you've lost some weight. And your cheeks are pale. Don't tell me that damned water in the Pump Room actually does some good, for I'll not believe it. Perhaps you're pale from all that mess they plastered on your face. But I must say, Mrs. Varley, tonight you look every day of the twenty-three years you claim to be."

She glared at him in the glass. He laughed at her expression, and Louisa suddenly realized just how glad she was to see him.

So glad, in fact, that she made no demur when he offered to walk her home. They trudged in silence for a bit and then he asked abruptly, "Who usually walks with you?"

"No one."

He stared at her in the light from a flickering gas street lamp. "Do you mean to tell me that you walk home at this hour by yourself? In this neighborhood? My God, woman, have you no notion of what could happen to you?"

"What I don't have is any choice," she answered wearily.

Lyston changed the subject abruptly. "Why were you demoted? I thought you played Desdemona very well."

"Were you there?" Louisa looked up at him in astonishment.

"Of course I was there. How else would I have formed an opinion of your ability—which, by the way, is a lot greater than I gave you credit for," he added grudgingly. "But certainly I was there. When I saw the playbill advertising a Mrs. Grayson in the part, I was curious. I'd begun to think that every female with my patronymic was on the stage."

"Oh, then you did not know I had come to London?" Louisa was inappropriately disappointed.

"How could I have known?" His brows went up. "You certainly did not confide your plans to me when you hared off and left me standing in front of the Pump Room in mid-sentence, as it were. What got into you, by the way? Was it something one of those gossip-mongers said?"

"I don't recall." Then to change the subject and keep her own perspective, she asked him, "How is the Honourable Miss Sedgwick?"

"Very well, thank you. She also is in London."

"And you're not dancing attendance?"

"I don't live in her pocket," he answered briefly. "She has a penchant for Almack's Assembly Rooms, while I find the place a deadly bore."

They had reached Louisa's house. She watched Lyston's aristocratic face as he surveyed its run-down appearance and looked with distaste over the disreputable neighborhood. "I thought you were supposed to have gone up in the world."

"So did I." She shrugged. "Please accept my thanks, Lord Lyston. I must say I did feel safer for your escort."

"Not quite so fast. I want to see the inside of this flea hostel. Please lead the way. Oh, come now, Mrs. Varley, no need to look so Friday-faced. I assure you, your virtue is safe enough."

The fellow lodger who passed them on the stairs obviously thought otherwise. She gave Louisa a telling look and sniffed as if to imply that "Her Ladyship" had joined her own ranks soon enough.

Lord Lyston did not miss the look. "Nice company you keep here," he muttered.

"Just what you might expect, in fact," she answered sweetly and smiled as he glowered at her.

Lyston stood speechless in the middle of Louisa's bedchamber and stared around in disbelief. Then he strode over and picked up the mousetrap she'd set by a likely-looking hole in the dingy baseboards. He shot a disgusted look at the corpus delicti dangling from it, opened her door again, and gave trap and mouse a heave. They stood in silence listening to it rattle and bounce its way down the stairs. "You can't go on living here," Lord Lyston said.

"Indeed, I can. In fact, I have no choice. I was led to believe I would soon get a rise in salary, and I'd hoped to move then. But in view of Mr. Kean's reaction to me . . ." She left the sentence incomplete.

"So that bastard was responsible for the change of parts."

"Yes. He doesn't like sharing the stage, it seems," Louisa answered wearily. "I'm planning to talk to the management of Covent Garden and see if I can get on there. It may help that the *Chronicle* spoke well of me." A note of pride crept in her voice.

"I read the notice," Lyston said, with a notable lack of interest.

"It was brief, I'll admit." Louisa was offended. "But it could help. Who knows? Of course I am under contract to Drury Lane, but under the circumstances, they will doubtlessly be glad to break it."

His lordship, obviously, was not concerned with her career plans. "Be that as it may, you can't continue living here. I have a house in Bloomsbury Square that's empty at the moment. You can go there. It's a comfortable walk to Drury Lane. Not bad for Covent Garden, either, if it comes to that."

She gave him a speaking look. "Oh, have no fear. I myself live in Brook Street."

"I did not mean that."

"Did you not?"

"It must be obvious to you that I cannot move into your house."

"It isn't obvious to me at all."

"In the first place, I'm quite at a loss to know why you should even make the offer."

"Altruism, I suppose." Her brows went up. "Oh, you think that impossible, do you? Well, then, I, too, am at a loss. Perhaps it's because I think that Adrian would turn in his grave to see you in such squalid circumstances."

Louisa smiled suddenly to herself. Adrian had assured her that his brother would take care of her. Of course, this was a far cry from what he'd had in mind. Lyston looked at her curiously. "Well?" he asked.

"How do you happen to own a house in Bloomsbury? Isn't that a far remove from Hyde Park?" she mocked.

"Far enough," he answered evenly. "If you must know, I bought it for a mistress. An ex-mistress, I might add."

"I'm glad to see that your betrothal has reformed you."

"Not at all. The lady turned out to be a crashing bore."

"How fortunate for the Honourable Miss Sedgwick."

"The Honourable Miss Sedgwick," his lordship retorted, "would hardly be inclined to concern herself with anything so trivial. But are we not straying from the point?"

"Are we? Perhaps that *is* the point."

He sighed impatiently. "If you are asking if I

have designs upon your virtue, the answer is no. If you are wondering if people will think that I have, the answer is that they are bound to. But it appears to me that living in this hellhole—that's obviously a brothel of the lowest type—has already sunk you below reproach." He frowned as he consulted her mantel clock. "At any rate it's rather late to shift you now. I'll send my carriage round tomorrow. And I trust you won't be too sap-skulled to take advantage of my offer. Of course if that mouse's relatives come back to look for it tonight—and they will most likely—I'm confident you'll see reason. In the meantime, I'm overdue at Watier's. Goodnight, Mrs. Varley."

Lord Lyston left Louisa staring after him open-mouthed as he closed the door.

Chapter
Thirteen

IT WAS WELL PAST THREE O'CLOCK BEFORE LOUISA FI-
nally fell asleep. She had convinced herself that
an evening spent at Watier's, an exclusive club for
gentlemen known for its deep play and the excel-
lence of its cellar, would drive her situation from
Lord Lyston's mind. Therefore she had no need to
reach a decision.

But at half-past eight, she heard a carriage stop
outside her house. Peering through the dingy window, she identified the equipage as Lord Lyston's,
its ownership advertised by the liveried coachman
and the crest upon its door. Louisa smiled in spite
of all her agitation. There was nothing surrepti-
tious about his lordship. He cared little what the
world might think.

Later on, when there was time to reconsider,
Louisa realized that she never actually decided
that she would move. She simply packed up her
things under the detached eye of his lordship's foot-

man and then preceded him out the door. Perhaps the predicted visit of the mouse relations spurred her on, or perhaps she came to the realization that she could not stand that dreadful place another day. Or perhaps the image of Adrian—"See, I told you Richard would come through"—prodded her into going. Whatever the motivation, Louisa sank back among the cushions of Lyston's well-sprung coach and reflected that once again her life had taken a new direction without her being responsible for the change. "I seem to have no control over my fate at all," she reflected with a tinge of bitterness.

The Bloomsbury house was charming. Louisa wondered whether the departed mistress could claim the credit or if his lordship had seen to the decor. The cook and housemaid who cared for it greeted her impassively. Louisa had little doubt that they were accustomed to such unconventional arrangements. In spite of all her resolutions not to be, she felt quite uncomfortable as she introduced herself to them.

No matter that her position was, to say the least, equivocal, Louisa found that her change of address soon improved her life. London lost its forbidding aspect and beckoned her. And on those days when she was free from Drury Lane, she became a tourist. With her guidebook in her hand, she visited the Tower, saw the Elgin marbles, gawked at Carlton House, and went to Vauxhall Gardens. And she spent many delightful hours in Henrietta Street browsing in Layton & Shears and in the other modish shops. She reveled in the profusion of French gloves, Indian muslins, tippets of fur, and all sorts of trimmings of the very latest crack, only rarely experiencing annoying twinges of regret that she had no money to purchase any of them.

One extravagance Louisa did allow herself proved to be a grave mistake. She hired a hackney coach to drive her through Hyde Park. She arrived at the hour of the fashionable promenade, when the members of the *ton* were out full force on horseback, in fancy carriages or "on the strut." Louisa was painfully conscious that she had invaded an alien world, now forever closed to her. And when she thought she spied Lord Lyston and the Honourable Miss Sedgwick tooling along smartly in a high-perch phaeton, she quickly directed the coachman to take her back to Bloomsbury Square.

The waste of money gnawed Louisa's conscience, for she was growing more and more concerned about her future. A visit to Covent Garden had proved disappointing. The theater manager seemed impressed both with her looks and her ability. "I read of your Desdemona in the *Chronicle*," he remarked, much to her gratification. And, without coming right out and saying so, he also made it plain that he realized the nature of her difficulties. "The problem is," he said, "we've got no openings. Later on, perhaps . . ." and he had bowed her politely out the door, destroying her hopes of bettering her position and making it possible to pay Lord Lyston sufficient rent to salvage her battered pride.

Just how long Louisa would be able to continue playing at Drury lane was anybody's guess. Her situation grew more difficult every day. Having deposed her from her throne as leading actress, Kean had been content to ignore Louisa for a while. But now she was receiving a great deal of unwelcome attention from the star. Indeed, she was becoming more and more hard pressed to avoid his lecherous gropings.

At first her air of gentility had given her immunity, for Kean preferred the lowest kind of company. Indeed, he kept a bevy of prostitutes hanging around the theater and was known to make use of their services in between the acts. This created some rather peculiar problems. It was always impossible to tell just how long the intervals would be. All depended upon how amorous the star was feeling at the time. Once when the harried stage manager asked if the intermission would be long, Kean answered, "Not this time." His venereal disease had called a halt to his usual dalliance.

Always, off the stage Kean's true haunts had been the taverns around Drury Lane. There he could set aside his various personae and be himself. There his baser nature was allowed full range. He could behave as badly as he chose among the broken-down actors, prostitutes, and criminals who were his only friends. But now wealth and genius were forcing him into another world. He was being courted by society and invited to the great houses to dine with the nation's fashionable. And in this exalted company he was tongue-tied and subdued, completely out of his element and resentful of a world that regarded him as a passing curiosity.

Now, to her alarm, Louisa became aware that Kean placed her in the category of those whom he pretended to despise but whose social superiority caused him to be consumed with envy. She feared that having her for a conquest might become necessary for his pride. And she truly believed him capable of taking her by force. Keeping Kean at bay would not be easy. Keeping him at bay and keeping her job as well might be impossible.

Then, just as abruptly as Kean's lecherous advances had begun, they stopped. At first Louisa was too relieved to wonder why. And then she understood. He had walked from the theater one evening to see Lord Lyston's footman there, waiting, as always, to walk her home. He evidently had made inquiries and reached the obvious conclusion: Louisa was Lyston's mistress. And not even Kean would risk offense where his lordship was concerned.

"If only he knew." Louisa smiled to herself without much humor and prayed that Kean would stay deceived. Then she went on to wonder if Lyston was aware that their names were being linked together. Probably not, she decided. For he had spoken the truth when he'd said he had no ulterior motives where she was concerned. He had not visited his Bloomsbury house even once during the entire month that she had lived there. That fact should have made her feel relieved; instead it left her with mixed feelings. Louisa had seen his lordship, though. She had peeped through the curtains at the audience one night before the play began and had spied him and Miss Sedgwick with a glittering party in the stage box. And for that performance she had played Emilia with rather more brilliance than was really prudent.

Perhaps then if it had happened sooner—right after she had moved into Lord Lyston's house, for instance—Louisa would not have been alarmed when late one night she heard a key rattling in the front-door lock. The footman had delivered her from the theater about an hour before. She was dressed for bed and in the act of snuffing the candles in the drawing room when she heard the noise. And she was all alone. The servants had retired some time ago to their quarters over the carriage house. Louisa looked wildly around to locate some weapon for defense. When Lord Lyston stepped across his threshold, he found her brandishing a poker and trying to look brave.

"Hardly the most welcoming of receptions," he remarked as he removed the black cape lined in white silk that he was wearing over his evening clothes. "It must be windy," Louisa thought inanely as she noted his tousled hair.

His lordship stood quite still and studied her intently. Even though her nightdress was quite demure and buttoned chastely to her chin, his stare contrived to make her feel that she was all but undressed before him. "I think you look more desirable right now than I've ever seen you," he finally said, quite matter-of-factly. "It's a bit hard to decide, though. You're always taking a chap's breath away—at the Theatre Royal for example, in that blue dress you wore. Oh, I could give you quite a number of instances when you looked more desirable than any other female I've ever seen. But, yes, I do think this tops them all. Or would—if you'd put that poker down." And he walked slowly toward Louisa, removed it from her nerveless fingers, propped it against the hearth, and took her into his arms.

This time there was no condemning stab of conscience when she did not struggle. Louisa recalled his first kiss too vividly to expect that she could or should do other than melt into his embrace. This second venture was even longer in duration and far more ardent. "Oh, I do love you," a voice breathed at its conclusion, and she realized with a wave of sadness that the voice was hers.

"Do you?" Lord Lyston answered huskily, tenderly pushing the hair back from her cheek while he held her close and gazed at her. "My God, Louisa, you're beautiful. I can't get my fill of looking at you. I've even taken to seeing you when you aren't there. Lord knows, no other woman has ever had this effect on me."

His nearness was intoxicating. Louisa felt quite

giddy, near to fainting, like some swooning gothic heroine. Then slowly, unwillingly, her brain began to function once again. She stiffened in his arms and sniffed. Brandy! The fumes were overpowering. No wonder she felt giddy! The secondhand effect was enough to send any but the strongest head to reeling. She peered up into his lordship's eyes. That melting look that she had taken to be passion now seemed open to new interpretation. Lord Lyston, though he hid it well, was clearly inebriated.

"You're foxed!" Louisa gasped indignantly.

"Certainly not!" He sounded injured. "A trifle up in the world, perhaps, but certainly not foxed."

"However you choose to term your condition, I think that you should leave now. We both seem to have lost our heads a bit. Your excuse can be the brandy. Mine must be fatigue and the lateness of the hour. At any rate, good night, Lord Lyston."

"Oh, no. I have no intention of leaving." And to prove his point Lyston sat down in a wing chair and stretched out his legs. Louisa continued to stand, and he stared up at her. "No, you'll not get rid of me so easily this time. I've decided to move in with you."

"I beg your pardon?" Louisa said icily.

"No need of that. You haven't offended me. In fact, the evening's gone quite well so far, I'd say. It could be improved though if you'd come sit here on my lap." He patted a muscular satin-clad leg invitingly.

"Lord Lyston." Louisa's voice was thick with anger. "I'll ask you again. Please go."

"Oh, I almost forgot." He reached into the recesses of his coat. "I'd hate to get off on the wrong foot with you—a beautiful, desirable actress from Drury Lane, Bath, Brussels—God knows where else. I wouldn't want to treat you like any light-skirt. Here." And he tossed a small box toward her. She caught and opened it in a cold fury, but gasped in spite of herself at the diamond earrings sparkling on their cushion of dark velvet. "It's gilding the lily for you to wear such gewgaws, I'll admit," Lyston remarked gallantly. "But women usually like that sort of thing, so I don't suppose you're any different."

"And to which of my predecessors did they belong?" Louisa inquired, a bit too sweetly. "Or do they get passed along from one to another with the house?"

His lordship looked offended. "Of course not. They're for you particularly. I just bought 'em on the way over when I decided to join you here. By the by, I didn't bring a nightshirt, but then I don't suppose I'll need it." He chuckled wickedly. He was, she noted almost dispassionately, very drunk indeed. "I can send William over for all that sort of thing tomorrow. Oh—nearly forgot. You were asking about the earrings. Of course they're for you. I found this jeweler cove who lives above his shop and threw rocks at his window until he opened up. Of course I wouldn't bring you used earrings." He sounded hurt.

"I'm relieved that you are not depriving the Honourable Miss Sedgwick of your family heirlooms."

"Naturally I would do no such thing." The very notion seemed to horrify Lord Lyston.

"Miss Sedgwick would be touched by your devotion to her interests," Louisa said with heavy sarcasm.

"Haven't we talked about this before?" He eyed her suspiciously. "Seems to me we have. Bound to have pointed out that Miss Sedgwick and I will have a marriage of convenience."

"With most of the convenience being yours, no doubt."

"Not necessarily." He was all injured innocence. "I don't care what she does as long as she's discreet about it." He choked suddenly. "Though demme if I can imagine any cove getting into that sort of taking over Letitia. Mind you, I think the world of her, of course. Damn fine woman on a horse. But must admit, she really doesn't have that sort of effect. She's not at all like you when it comes to that. Too much breeding, I suspect. Now take you—you fairly bowl a man right off his pins. The first time he sees you, he's a goner. All he can think about is making love to you. But then, of course, you know all that better than I do. Good God, just check your record. There's me, of course—and Kean—and Adrian—oh, dear God, Adrian!" His voice broke. "The poor boy must have been hit harder even than I am, and I wouldn't have thought such a thing was possible. But by God he must have been. The boy meant to marry you."

"*Did* marry me." Louisa barely managed to get out the words.

"No, not really. Unless you're counting what may have happened between you before that illegal ceremony. And I really think Adrian was too honorable for that sort of thing."

"Unlike you."

"God, yes. Unlike me. Adrian was a far better sort of chap." Louisa thought Lyston would burst into tears and watched in fascinated horror. But he got a grip upon himself and continued his catalog. "Let's see now, besides the besotted Grayson brothers, there's Kean—and, of course, that chap you lived with so long in Brussels—mustn't forget him, must we? What was his name?"

"Varley." Louisa was numb now past all feeling, frozen and lost.

"Yes, the mysterious Varley. Lady Follett tells me you lived quite openly with him in Belgium." He looked at her accusingly. "You know what's wrong with you, Louisa? The thing that really confuses a chap? You simply do not look the type. That's why I said what I said when I said it, and why I'm going back on my word now." He stopped a moment and thought a bit. "Don't recall ever having gone back on my word before, actually. Not a gentlemanly thing to do. But that's just the point we've been discussing. You're no lady, though you certainly could fool the world on that score if you'd a mind to. But then, you're an actress. I have to keep reminding myself of that. Fooling the world is your profession. But anyhow I haven't forgot I told you when I offered you this house that I didn't intend to—you know. God knows I wanted to. But in the first place it seemed incestuous—Adrian and all, only you never did with him, now did you?—and besides, Adrian's d-dead." Again he barely stopped himself from miring down in despondency and resumed his drunken rambling. "But the real reason I didn't is that I didn't think you'd stand for it. My mistake. But I just explained all that before, didn't I? About you looking more like a lady than a light-skirt. Have I offended you by that word?" he inquired suddenly.

"Indeed, no," Louisa answered icily. " '*In vino veritas*,' as they say."

"In wine, truth," he translated admiringly. "That's exactly what I mean about you, Louisa. I mean to say, your average Cyprian doesn't go in for Latin quotations. Only to set the record straight, it's brandy I've been drinking, and not wine. You don't happen to have any more around here, do you? I rather thought not."

"I think you're straying from the point. You were about to tell me why you changed your mind about offering me *carte blanche.*"

"Kean, of course. My God, Louisa—how could you? That Godawful little cit. After Adrian." He looked ill. "Oh, I know he's a brilliant actor and all that, and I suppose he can do you a lot of good in that department—but really, Louisa. It's not a thing I even like to think about. You letting that rake touch you." He closed his eyes as though to blot out the picture his words had evoked. "I don't mind saying it nearly put me off you. Which goes to show how far gone I am about you, or it would have. As it is, I don't care much for myself though," he continued candidly. "Standards and all that."

"And just what gave you the idea that I have allowed Mr. Kean to 'touch me,' as you so euphemistically describe it?"

He laughed drunkenly. " 'Euphemistically.' That's nearly as good as *'In vino veritas.'* 'Pon my soul, you could beat out an Almack patroness when it comes to being high in the instep, and that's a fact. I got the idea that Mr. Kean touched you 'euphemistically,' " he parroted, "because he told me so."

"He what!"

"I told you he was a cit and not a gentleman. Despicable thing to do."

"Kean told you that he'd made love to me?" Louisa stared at him in horror.

"Actually, the way he delicately put it was, 'We have something in common, Lord Lyston, so I understand. We are sharing the same mistress.' "

"And just when did this conversation take place?" Louisa had not thought she could feel any more degraded. She knew now that she'd been wrong.

"Didn't I tell you? A bit ago. At one of Byron's boring suppers. He's been lionizing Kean, you know—who lionizes him in turn. A pair of widgeons if I ever saw them. Anyway, Kean was even more cast away than I am now, and he leaned across the table and said what he said, and I threw my brandy in his face and left. Pity about the brandy. Are you sure there's none around here? Well, never mind. But anyhow, when I left I got to thinking that if that's the kind of life you lead, then I might just as well go ahead and forget about Adrian and get you out of my system once and for all. For actually you have been bothering me a lot more than I'd care to admit if I was entirely sober, you see, Louisa."

"And you believed him?"

"Believed him?" Lord Lyston considered the question for the first time, evidently. "I must have," he answered reasonably, "or why else would I have bought the earrings and shown up here? I mean to say it was a caddish enough thing for him to have said if it was true. Unthinkable if it wasn't."

"Yes, quite unthinkable. But let me be very sure I have this straight. You have come to offer me *carte blanche* and would not have done so except that Mr. Kean has now sunk me below reproach."

"Something like that, only demme if I know whether Kean has spurred me on or put me off."

"And the diamond earrings are to be my payment?"

"They're a gift," Lyston said reproachfully. "A bauble. A token of my esteem."

" 'Esteem,' " she echoed bitterly. "You certainly have a way with words."

"Esteem—affection—whatever." He looked morose. "The problem is, nothing seems to fit what I

161

feel for you. What should I have said? Please accept this gift, Mrs. Varley, as a token of my obsession?"

"And another thing. My name is not Varley."

"Well, it ain't Grayson either. Just who are you, Louisa? Come to think on it, I really don't know a damned thing about you, do I?"

"You seem to know all that you require. But I think this conversation has gone on for far too long. Not being of the leisure class, I have to be at the theater tomorrow. Now, if you'll excuse me, I'm going to bed."

"Excuse you? I'm coming with you. That's the whole idea—the diamonds and all. How could you have forgot so soon?"

"Just careless I suppose." And while he hauled himself rather unsteadily to his feet, Louisa darted into her bedchamber, closed the door, and locked it.

Lord Lyston, who had come weaving after her, tried the knob, paused a moment, then rattled it until Louisa feared the door might part company with its hinges. "I say, Louisa," he called, "the damned thing's stuck."

"It's locked, Lord Lyston. Now if you truly wish to sleep here, may I suggest you try the drawing-room settee?"

There was a longer pause while his lordship seemed to be turning things over in his mind. "Louisa"—his voice was a bit thicker than the door—"does this mean you're turning down my offer of *carte blanche*?"

"It does."

"Oh." Another pause. "If you think to hold out for marriage, it won't do. Quite above your touch, you know. 'Lyston of Graylands' and all that."

"I know." In spite of herself, Louisa smiled a little grimly.

"Besides, there's Miss Sedgwick. Betrothed, you know."

"I know. Now do be quiet and go to sleep."

"Be a good fellow, Louisa, and let me in."

"Good night, Lord Lyston." Louisa stood there by the door for several seconds. Then she slowly walked to the four-poster, blew out the candle, and lay down upon her bed.

Chapter Fourteen

FOR SOME TIME LOUISA LAY AWAKE LISTENING TO Lord Lyston stumbling through the house. Then, when all seemed quiet, she went back into the withdrawing room. He had ignored her suggestion of the settee and was sprawled in the wing chair, his mouth slightly ajar and his arms dangling limply across the chair rests. She looked at him clinically, wondering just how much brandy he had consumed and thinking with remarkable detachment that if she found him appealing in his present state, she really was past praying for. He did not rouse as she banked the fire and placed an afghan over him.

Louisa stood a moment and stared at the diamonds which sparkled in their box from the light of a guttering candle. Then, seeming to come to a conclusion, she picked up the case. Extinguishing the tiny flame flickering feebly in its pool of tallow, she went back to bed.

Louisa was up early next morning, moving quietly in her room so as not to disturb Lord Lyston's slumber. But when she walked into the drawing room with her portmanteau in her hand, she saw that all the care she'd taken had been unnecessary. A fox hunt through the house would hardly have disturbed his lordship. He was breathing heavily, dead to the world. She thought with pleasure of the headache he was bound to have when he awakened and with regret that she'd not be there to witness it.

Even so, to take no chances, Louisa set her bag down softly before seating herself at the rosewood writing table. For a moment she chewed the tip of her quill thoughtfully, then wrote:

My dear Lord Lyston,

I regret that I find myself unable to fall in with the scheme for my future which you proposed last night. I am sure, though, that you will soon find a more satisfactory replacement for me.

However, as you may by now have noticed, I have accepted that 'token of affection' which you kindly offered me. Not a sporting thing to do perhaps; let's just say that I consider it a part of Adrian's provision for my future. I think he would have wished it. He was, after all, the only true gentleman I have ever met.

After a moment's further thought she signed it "Louisa Grayson," sprinkled it with sand to dry the ink, then walked over to the wing chair and placed it carefully on the chest of the sleeping Lyston. She then picked up her portmanteau and left the house.

Louisa's first destination was a pawnbroker's shop. Her second stop was Drury Lane, where she handed in her resignation to a not-too-regretful Mr. Arnold. A little later, she was on the public coach for Bath, only vaguely bothered by the fact that she had had so little compunction in disposing of Lord Lyston's property. Nor did she expect her next step to disturb her conscience very much. And, indeed, if her conscience should assert itself and rise up to plague her, Louisa felt quite sure that the recollection of only a few of the things Lyston had said to her the night before would silence it forever. *"In vino veritas"* indeed! Her eyes flashed angrily. Revenge could never blot out his words, nor soothe entirely their scorpion sting. But it would help. Oh, definitely it would help.

Her first stop in Bath was a solicitor's office. The man hemmed and hawed and suggested that, even though he could see no problem with the legality of her documents, it might be that his lordship could build a case on the fact that his brother was at the point of death—*"non compos mentis,"* you might say; the marriage had not been consummated—and so on. He thought that she might do well not to act in haste. Perhaps some kind of settlement might be reached.

"I do not wish a settlement," Louisa interrupted firmly. "What I wish is to take possession of my late husband's home tomorrow, and I wish you to make the necessary arrangements for my doing so."

"Tomorrow!" He was aghast.

"Tomorrow," she said firmly. "I intend to arrive at Graylands tomorrow afternoon. I do not wish that arrival to be a shock."

"But I believe Lord Lyston is in London," he protested.

"Good. Then he won't add to the confusion, will he?" Louisa stood up. "Don't forget that the house was the property of my late husband. Lord Lyston has no call to concern himself."

It was disappointing to discover that the Scopeses

were away on tour. "Business fell off, you see, after you left them, dear," Mrs. Bottoms informed her. "They're keeping their rooms here, though, and I'm certain Miss Scopes wouldn't mind you using hers. That other actress left them, and I've let the room you and she had to a retired gentleman who's here to take the waters." There was something about the coy way that Mrs. Bottoms imparted this bit of information that made Louisa suspect a romance was in the making. She certainly hoped so. It was time someone she knew had a bit of luck.

The next day, Louisa was tempted to walk to Graylands. But the impropriety of arriving dusty and on foot convinced her more than the weight of her portmanteau to hire a rig and coachman to take her there. It was late afternoon when she entered the door of her new home.

As it turned out, Louisa found taking possession of the Dower House to be rather flat. She had expected some high drama—perhaps a bailiff standing on the steps ready to repel her. Instead she was greeted by the solicitor, who had handed her a set of keys. "I think the butler up in the big house may have apoplexy," he said dryly. "Good job of work that I brought the sheriff with me. Wasn't sure we were going to get the old fellow to part with these even then. He was bound and determined that nothing should be done in his lordship's absence. I finally convinced him that you weren't likely to set the place on fire or anything like that before Lord Lyston was in residence. And besides, as the sheriff pointed out, the house *did* belong to your dear, departed husband anyhow. All the same, I'll bet a monkey there's a footman haring it up to London this very minute."

"I wouldn't dream of wagering against you." Louisa smiled without much humor. "But I thank you for all your trouble." She pulled some banknotes from her reticule and handed them to the solicitor. "I do hope this finishes our business. But if we have to go to court, I'll call on you again."

The solicitor gave the definite impression that he hardly relished such a possibility. No doubt he did not consider her generous fee adequate compensation for offending the county's leading citizen, Louisa thought. She herself just might relish tangling with the great Lord Lyston.

Louisa was given a full day's grace before the crisis came. But when she blew out her candle for her second night's sleep in the Dower House, she could see the lights blazing from the windows in the Hall. His lordship had doubtless returned. Louisa planned to be very much the lady of the house, cool, poised, and quite aloof, perhaps pouring tea in the withdrawing room, when he came looking for her.

Instead, Lord Lyston walked into the basement early the next morning to find her smeared with soot, trying to coax a fire to burn in the kitchen fireplace underneath a kettle meant for tea. His footsteps right behind her made her drop the fire tongs with a shriek. "Don't you believe in knocking?" she asked him crossly.

"That's only one of the hazards of occupying someone else's property," he retorted, taking over the firemaking with remarkable efficiency.

"How did you know how to do that?" She was incensed by the injustice of it all. "You have servants who even sneeze for you, I understand."

"Just natural aptitude, I suppose." He looked her over critically. "You, on the other hand, don't appear cut out for house-napping."

"I've done remarkably well, I think. If you'd taken the trouble to look at the house before, you could see the transformation. I worked myself to

168

the bone making the place habitable. It's just that I'm not terribly good at fires."

"So I see. Wash your face, why don't you, while I fill this kettle."

Things were not going at all the way she'd planned. Louisa felt she'd been put to a quite unfair disadvantage when it was Lord Lyston who made the tea. He poured it out into two cups upon the kitchen table for all the world as though they were the butler and the housemaid taking a cozy break.

"What do you have to go with it?" he inquired and looked appalled when she brought out the Sally Lunn she'd baked the day before. It had been barely edible even then. His lordship took a bite and grimaced. "Brought this over from Waterloo then, did you? Whose ammunition was it, ours or theirs?"

"I did not invite you to breakfast, you may remember. You might have waited till a proper hour for morning calls. Why don't you simply march back up the hill and ask your army of servants to prepare—"

"Your mind certainly seems to dwell upon my household staff," he interrupted.

"Yes, I suppose it does," Louisa answered glumly. "All of which reminds me, I've a great deal to do today, including stocking my bare larder. And since I don't think you're paying me a social call, let's get to the point. Why are you here, Lord Lyston?"

He reached for the teapot and refilled their cups. She glared at his preemption of her hostess role. "I've come to apologize," he said.

"I beg your pardon?"

"I said I've come to apologize. What did you think? That I've come here to evict you?"

"The thought had crossed my mind."

"I've no intention of doing so."

"Which is just as well, for my solicitor tells me that you could not."

"Then your solicitor is obviously a jackass. But let's not get into a wrangle over legalities. As I've said, I've no plans to throw you out."

Louisa looked at him suspiciously. "Now am I supposed to grovel in gratitude for what is legally mine?"

"No, you are not." He glared. "I'm merely stating that I'm through chasing you from houses—no matter who the owner is. You're making this damned difficult, you know. Here I'm the one who's groveling for my shabby conduct—"

"Groveling!" In spite of herself, Louisa giggled. "I must confess I'd love to see it, but I suspect that such activity is well beyond your range. In fact I'm sure it is, if that's what you think you're doing now."

"Don't judge too quickly. I really haven't gotten properly started yet. Mrs. Varley, I sincerely regret the despicable things I said to you the other night and hope you will forgive me for them. I was very, very drunk, or I would not have behaved so reprehensibly." He paused in the midst of what was obviously a rehearsed speech to offer this aside, "By the by—what you said in your note about Adrian being the only gentleman you've met, that stung a bit."

"It was intended to. I suppose that concludes our business, then." She stood up and removed their cups and saucers.

"Does it? There's no need to dismiss me quite so cavalierly."

"Oh, is there not?" Louisa wheeled on him. "What am I supposed to do now? Accept your apology? Thank you for allowing me to stay here? Well, I'll do neither. You've shown nothing but contempt for me from the time we met. And drunk or sober, you've made it plain that you consider me a light-skirt of the lowest class."

"I never said of the lowest class," Lyston snarled back, beginning to grow as angry now as she.

"Oh, no? There seems to be no depravity you do not think me capable of. Edmund Kean indeed!"

"Damn it, Louisa, I said I was sorry. The moment I sobered up, I knew that could never have been so. Then, when I went to Drury Lane looking for you, the manager said you'd gone. His theory was that you'd run away from Kean's advances."

"So it was really Mr. Arnold who cleared my name, and not your better judgement."

"No, confound it! He simply confirmed what I already knew. Stop it, Louisa!"

"Am I making you uncomfortable?"

"You're giving it your best."

"Well, it's a petty sort of revenge for the way you've blackened my character, but I'm glad of it. Now if you'll excuse me, Lord Lyston, as I pointed out, I've a great deal to do."

"Louisa, let me finish!" he thundered. "I came down here to tell you that none of what's happened seems to matter. God knows I've put up one devil of a fight, but I never seemed to stand a chance, no matter what I learned about you—my own brother, for God's sake; that scoundrel you lived with in Belgium. Why, even if it had turned out that you'd made love to that strutting actor—don't get on your high ropes, I know you haven't—I doubt it would have changed a thing. Nothing seems to make any difference in how I feel about you. And I'm through with fighting it. Louisa, will you marry me?"

She had been placing their tea things in a pan

for washing up, but she turned slowly now to face him. "Did I hear you right?" she inquired softly.

"Yes. I'm asking you to marry me."

"Oh. And I suppose I'm expected to leap at the chance."

"You might, yes."

"Give me one good reason why I should."

"*One* reason. My God, Louisa, if you can't see the advantage—"

"Rather like Cinderella, in fact. Right out of the ashes straight into the arms of her Prince Charming."

His eyes narrowed at her sarcasm. "I'm well aware I'm no Prince Charming—nor would I wish to be—but otherwise, there's some parallel."

"Oh, yes, indeed. I understand you're a regular nabob. By the by, I pawned the trinkets you gave me. You can redeem them, if you like. Tell me, though, would you be as generous to a wife as to a mistress? Men generally are not, so I've been told."

"I doubt you'd find much reason to complain," he answered haughtily.

"No, guttersnipe that I am, I should not think so. But all the same, I do not think I am for sale."

"I never supposed you were."

"Oh, no? I thought that was the thrust of your proposal. It certainly was for your London proposition."

"How many times do I have to say that was the brandy talking? But I was not so foxed as to miss your end of the conversation. That's why I thought you might not be so averse to marrying me as you now appear to be."

"Indeed? And why would you think that?"

"You said you loved me."

Louisa dropped her eyes before the intensity of

172

his gaze. "Did I actually say that? I really don't re-call."

"You did. And I think you damn well do recall it."

She forced herself to look him in the eye. "If I did say such a foolish thing, I must have been throwing myself into the scene. I am an actress, don't forget."

"I'm not likely to."

"Oh, and by the by—to set the record straight—just what did you intend doing about your other fiancée? I don't know if I've ever mentioned this, but I've become rather bored by proposals from men who are already committed elsewhere." She glared at him, and he glared back.

"Naturally I intend to break off my betrothal—or rather, to give Miss Sedgwick the opportunity to do so."

"How gentlemanly!" Louisa sneered. "But you need not bother on my account. I have no intention of marrying you."

Lord Lyston had gone rather white. "Louisa, I'm sorry if I botched this."

"Botched it?" She laughed lightly. "How could you possibly think so? Just because you said you'd lost the battle with your conscience and are now ready to sacrifice all your principles and finer feelings and make me your wife? What female would not be thrilled at such a romantic offer?"

"Would it have been better to lie to you? You can't expect me to rejoice over your unconventional past. You must know that our divergent backgrounds hardly make this the ideal union."

"If I had not known it, you've certainly pointed out often enough that men like you only offer *cartes blanches* to females like me. Well, now I've turned you down on both accounts. It would seem we have no more to say to one another."

"Evidently not." He was struggling for self-

173

control. "I don't suppose it would help at this point to go down on one knee and talk a lot of fustian about having longed to make the two of us one since first we met, or about wishing to give you the protection of my name—all the usual rot."

"No, it would not. Besides, you seem to forget, I already have your name."

"That you have not," he snapped. "There's no way I'll accept your marriage to my brother."

"So we've gone full circle," Louisa answered wearily. "We're back to my legal right to this house again. Well, I'm prepared to fight you for it."

"That will not be necessary. I meant it when I said I'd no intention of chasing you out of any other residences. And since you've made it plain that you prefer this one to the Hall, let me wish you joy of it. Now, if you'll forgive me for taking up so much of your valuable time." Lyston bowed mechanically, without really looking at her, and went striding from the room. Louisa heard the front door close with a slam that seemed to echo finality.

She sank down at the kitchen table where he had sat, then laid her head down upon her arms.

Chapter Fifteen

LOUISA'S SPIRITS WERE SOON LOWERED EVEN FARTHER. About an hour later, she heard a tapping at the rear entrance to the house. She had spent some time splashing her face with cold water after her bout of weeping, but as she checked in the glass before leaving her bedroom, she could see that the results had been almost negligible.

Louisa opened the servant's door to admit a fresh-faced couple. "We're Katie and Joe Moss, ma'am," the young man said, snatching off his cap. "His lordship sent us down to help you out."

"But I don't understand." Louisa faltered.

Katie chimed in helpfully. "His lordship said we was to say as how we're a couple that merely sneezes for him—that you'd know what he means, which is more'n we do—and that we'd be more use down here than up at the Hall."

"But I'm afraid I can't afford to pay you."

They both looked shocked. "Oh, his lordship does

that, ma'am. We can go right on living in the Hall, of course, but his lordship did say as how we could stay here at nights, too, if you was to want us."

"That won't be necessary. I wouldn't want to—" Louisa paused as she thought she detected a look of disappointment on their faces. "Unless, of course, you'd actually prefer it?"

It seemed they would indeed prefer it. "It being more quiet-like." Then with a little probing Louisa discovered that the two had been married for only a month and were chafing under the crowded conditions of the servants' hall. She was glad that she could make someone happy by her presence here— even if it meant accepting Lyston's charity.

Louisa marveled at the way the young couple went cheerfully about the job of making the Dower House habitable. Their efficiency made a mockery of all her efforts. Nevertheless, she was almost sorry she was robbed of the necessity of struggling with her own domestic problems. Hard work might have served as an antidote for the gloom her spirits had sunk into. Perhaps a walk. Louisa quickly decided against that course for fear she might encounter Lyston. But the threat of that was soon removed by an afterthought from Joe.

"Excuse me, ma'am." He came into the morning room where she was making some desultory stabs through an embroidery hoop. "I almost forgot. His lordship said as how you was to make free use of the stables. He drove the curricle up to London, but you're more than welcome to use the other rigs, he said."

As Joe went back to work, Louisa brooded. That Lyston was determined to kill her with kindness was evident. But to what purpose, she did not know. Not to further his suit, obviously, or why leave for London? The only conclusion was that his better judgment had once more got the upper hand, and he regretted his rashness of the day before.

Lord Lyston could not regret it as much as she. Louisa had long since recognized the fact that she was in love with him. So why then had she thrown his marriage offer in his face? It was more than even she could understand.

From pride, of course, she finally acknowledged. She was her father's daughter—no mistake. Some instinct had warned her that it would be just as humiliating to be wed against Lyston's better judgment as to have been married for her father's wealth and power.

Louisa told herself that she was behaving childishly. All she had to do was tell Lyston who her father was and explain the circumstances of her disastrous marriage to set everything to rights. But still she could not bring herself to do so. He had accepted Lady Follett's version of her character from the very first and had never wavered from his original opinion. Though he had fallen in love with her, he felt degraded by it. His marriage proposal had obviously taken a high toll from his self-esteem. Others might consider the offer a proof of real devotion, but Louisa definitely did not. She believed she recognized sexual infatuation when she saw it, and on the whole considered his offer of a *carte blanche* the more honorable of his two proposals.

Louisa did not doubt that he would shortly be over his obsession. She did not think it likely she'd be so fortunate. But now her immediate problem was to try and find some direction for her life. She'd been spinning rudderless long enough.

After reaching this conclusion, Louisa still seemed incapable of settling upon a course of action. She'd made her defiant, futile gesture. She'd occupied the Dower House and gotten away with it.

Now she knew she should not continue living there. But still she stayed.

She took long, tiring tramps around the estate, trying not to notice the curious glances of the workers. And, after vowing not to do so, she did avail herself of Lyston's stables, riding breakneck through the fields, splashing across streams, and jumping hedges, hoping to jolt herself out of the doldrums. Nothing worked. And then one day Louisa faced the fact that she was really marking time, hoping against hope that Lyston would return to Graylands. Three weeks passed, however, and he did not come. Obviously he was well ensconced in London and had by now buried his folly and taken up his old life where he'd abandoned it.

She must do the same. Work was the classic cure for being blue-deviled. After all, she had a profession to fall back upon. Drury Lane was not the last theater in the world. By now, surely, the Scopeses must have returned to Bath. She would have the mare saddled and ride in to see.

Louisa was quite touched by her Trim Street reception. Aunt Nell gave a delighted squeal then jumped up from the table where they were taking luncheon to plant a wet smack upon Louisa's cheek. Mr. Scopes pumped her hand up and down enthusiastically while his eyelids blinked a joyous accompaniment. Jem gave her a shy, glad smile and blushed. "Deuced glad to see you back," he managed at last to say.

Nothing would do but she must sit at table with them, help herself to tea and scones, and tell them all about her Drury Lane adventures. The Scopeses were especially full of questions about the great Edmund Kean. They listened with awe to Louisa's description of his prowess, then laughed and looked scandalized by turns at her anecdotes about his off-stage personality.

"Well, they certainly treated you shabbily!" Aunt Nell pronounced indignantly at the end of her recital.

"No worse than anyone else gets treated who plays on the same stage with Kean. I was foolish, I suspect, not to stick it out. But frankly, I'd had my fill. Besides, I was homesick."

What she had said was true. Still Louisa felt somewhat ashamed for hiding the more compelling reason. "I don't suppose you have a job for me?" she asked tentatively. "I know you've employed a new leading lady. I wouldn't expect to replace her, of course."

"As to that—" Mr. Scopes looked uncomfortable—"the girl we took on up and left us flat in Brighton—ran off with a guardsman there. Of course we'd love to have you. But the thing is, we've got nothing much to offer at the moment."

"There is the private theatrical," Aunt Nell chimed in. "That's something at any rate. And the money's not bad."

Mr. Scopes looked more and more distressed. "But Aunt Nell, you forget. Louisa has played with Kean!"

Louisa laughed. "Yes, and got demoted for my pains. I'm certainly not proud. Indeed, I found London to be most humbling. So, if you've a place for me in this private theatrical, I'll take it gladly."

Indeed, they had a place. In fact, Mr. Scopes had been at his wit's end wondering how to fill it. "The engagement's at a country estate belonging to a Sir Peter Farnsworth," he explained. "It's about twenty miles from here. He's having a large party in for the hunting and wants some evening entertainment. Who knows? If they like us, it could mean

179

more than one night's work. I understand the theater there is unexceptionable. Almost professional, in fact."

Louisa could well believe it. It was not at all unusual for great houses to have their own theaters. She herself had first acted in private theatricals upon her father's stage. The usual thing was to stage productions that were entirely amateur. Occasionally a few professionals were added to carry the main parts. But Sir Peter Farnsworth wished to entertain his guests, not involve them. So the Scopes Company would be entirely on its own.

After a lengthy discussion about the choice of play, followed by arrangements for rehearsals, Louisa rose reluctantly to leave. She'd found the Scopeses to be a tonic. She did not look forward now to country solitude.

Jem, who had remained silent during most of the animated conversation in the dining room, walked outside with her.

"Don't do it, Louisa," he blurted.

"I don't know what you mean." She looked at his troubled face uneasily.

"Don't come along on this private theatrical booking. It ain't at all what you might think."

"But I don't understand. It all sounds perfectly respectable."

"Well, it ain't. Oh, the people there will be the nobs, all right. All fit to take tea with the King, if the poor chap don't happen to be in a straitjacket at the time. But it's not drama they're interested in, it's making sport."

"Making sport? Jem, I've no idea what you're trying to say."

"It's just that these swells find it really entertaining to get a troupe like us—they could pay for the best, you know, right off the Theatre Royal stage—or London, for that matter. But that's not what they want at all. They want the worst." He grimaced bitterly. "And that's us, all right. They think it's larks to drink their port till they're good and bosky and then to heckle the poor sapskulls who are trying to perform. A lot more fun, mind you, than watching Kemble, for instance, do Macbeth up brown."

"Surely you're mistaken."

"I wish I was. We played one place like that already. And we've heard other companies talk about some private parties they've tried to act in front of. Fair curl your hair, it would. Well, like Auntie said, the money's good enough. And it's not so bad for the likes of us. But I don't want you messed up in it. You're a real actress, Louisa. And what's more, you're a lady."

"Thank you very much, Jem. But I'm a part of the Scopes Company, too. And if the rest of you can put up with such behavior, so can I. But surely it won't happen. Your father would have said so if he expected trouble."

"My father's a ninnyhammer." Young Jem sighed for the shortcomings of the elderly. "He thinks that just because old Farnsworth has a 'Sir' before his name that everything will be right and proper. But I know better."

He helped Louisa mount, and she smiled down at him. "Well, let's hope you're wrong. At any rate, don't look so blue-deviled, Jem. We're veterans. Remember Brussels? Surely there's not an audience this side of the Channel that can be as bad as that."

In spite of Jem's gloomy predictions of disaster, in the days that followed, Louisa found her spirits picking up. For the production gave her a purpose—and something to think about besides the absent

Lyston. It had been decided that, instead of tackling heavy drama, as Mr. Scopes had first proposed, they'd do a talking version of *Mother Goose*, usually done in pantomime. Not only would this take a minimum of rehearsal on their part, but it was also, they thought, well suited to complement a light-hearted house-party atmosphere. Also, Louisa decided privately, if the audience was disposed to be uncivil as Jem prophesied, the lighter play would not point up their dramatic shortcomings quite so clearly as coping with the Bard might do. Surely this would forestall ridicule.

Louisa was to play Columbine. Jem flushed with pleasure upon learning that he'd be Harlequin. "You're taller than Louisa now," Aunt Nell said with satisfaction, "and that means you're taller than Edmund Kean. He'd best look to his laurels if he knows what's good for him." Since the two of them were the mainstays of the production, they did most of the rehearsing, leaving it up to luck and the doubtful professionalism of the supporting players to carry off the evening. And, with a bit of added luck, they'd arrive at Farnsworth Hall early enough to set up scenery and have a full-cast runthrough.

The company made the trip in a hackney-chaise. Their expenses were covered grudgingly by Sir Peter Farnsworth. Paying the fare was preferable, he finally decided, to lodging a troupe of actors overnight. Besides Louisa and the Scopeses, there were two other players who, like the manager and Aunt Nell, were to do the stage work as well as play the smaller parts. The bumpy coach was crowded to the bursting point with all the paraphernalia necessary for a production. Louisa recalled with a sigh the well-sprung, roomy equipage of Baron Lyston. But the enthusiasm of her fellow players on what to them was a luxurious outing, plus the beauty of the autumn countryside, more than compensated for any discomfort she was experiencing.

Even Louisa was impressed by their first sight of Farnsworth Hall. Her companions were shocked into awed silence. The house was not so large as Graylands, Louisa noted, but to her way of thinking, it was by far the more attractive. The main house, built of the lovely stone indigenous to the area, was simplicity itself: three stories high, with windows in graduated proportions, reaching almost from floor to ceiling on the bottom story, of a medium height upon the second, and shorter still upon the third. Arches fanned the center door and the center window of the second story. A wing, added on at some later date in the style of Robert Adam, saved the house from severity.

"The theater must be in there." Mr. Scopes blinked toward the direction of Louisa's gaze.

"Bound to be," Aunt Nell murmured, still subdued by all the grandeur.

Following the instructions of their employer, they circled the house and pulled up in front of what Louisa did not doubt was the tradesmen's entrance. Kean and Kemble might be escorted through the front door of the mansion, but their little troupe rated no such courtesy.

An officious footman met them and whisked them down a hall into the theater. He rather grudgingly offered tea. Mr. Scopes, more awed than ever, seemed on the point of declining the inhospitable suggestion. Aunt Nell, though, was making a quick recovery. "Tea's in our contract," she said loftily, "and a high tea at that."

While the footman stalked off to discharge his mission, the thespians looked around them. The theater, though small, was far superior—especially in its decor—to any commercial ones the troupe had played in. Gilt paint and ornate plasterwork abounded. An enormous crystal chandelier hung over the auditorium. The pit, containing a raised wooden platform surmounted by rows of benches, would seat at least a hundred, Louisa guessed. For additional seating, a balcony curved around the room. Mr. Scopes saw her staring at it. "They won't be using that tonight," he said. "Should make our work a bit easier."

Louisa nodded gratefully. She had already noted how hollow their voices sounded in the hall, which made her fear that more attention had been given to ornamentation than to acoustics. Of course a crowd would help. Louisa wondered how large their audience would be. There was nothing more dismal than playing to a nearly empty house.

The footman settled that question for them when he returned with his lackeys and a laden tea cart. "There are only thirty guests staying in the house." He was rather smug, Louisa thought, with his use of "only." "However, some seventy-five persons will view the play."

"Anyone important here?" Aunt Nell asked the question as much to irritate the top-lofty footman as from a desire to know.

"Certainly." Louisa smiled to herself as she watched the struggle going on in the servant's mind: whether to snub these upstart actors or puff up the household's consequence. The latter inclination won, and he began to recite the guest list, which he informed them included the great names of Somerset.

But for Louisa, his listing quickly took on a nightmare quality, like a dream dreamed after some indigestible late-night supper, too fantastic to be taken seriously because one would surely soon

184

awaken. If she had drawn up a list herself of all the people she was most desperate to avoid, she thought, amazed at her detachment, the only one now missing would be Varley. And before the evening was over, she continued, he might just come strolling in.

"Lord and Lady Follett" was certainly a jolt. "Lord Lyston and his betrothed, the Honourable Letitia Sedgwick" made Louisa turn a little pale and sit down rather suddenly. But there was worse to follow. "Lord Faircot, who is from Yorkshire, but now resides in Bath for reasons of his health." This bit of news contrived to send the auditorium reeling.

"Well, I have no reason to hide from anyone," Louisa thought stoutly while cravenly wondering if her makeup might disguise her effectively. "I'm here to perform, and perform is what I'll do." She stopped herself in time from adding a fifth lump of sugar to her tea, then angrily pushed the cup aside along with thoughts of anything else except the play. Louisa joined her fellow performers on the stage to do a quick walk-through.

From the very first, fate seemed to conspire against them. Curtain time was scheduled for eight o'clock. But it was nearer nine before the guests began to file noisily into the theater. And it was obvious that their host had not stinted their supply of spirits. Indeed, some of the revelers still held wineglasses in their hands and waved them gaily at one another.

Louisa had long since traded off her nervousness for impatience. Her main fear now was that this lack of caring might be fatal to her performance. She stood with Jem upon the stage peering through the curtain crack at the boisterous audience as they found their seats. On the principle that a wise army scouts its enemy, she sought to locate the people in the group she dreaded most to see.

Her father was the easiest to find. He was being pushed into the auditorium in an invalid chair by one of his own servants. In spite of all their stormy past history, Louisa felt a surge of pity as the footman situated Lord Faircot's chair in the third-row aisle, then left to go stand against the wall and await a summons. She wondered if he could not walk at all, then noted the ornate stick at rest beside him in the chair.

Next she spotted Lady Follett bustling down the aisle with a small, cowed little man in tow, who must surely be Viscount Follett.

Then Louisa spied Lord Lyston and forgot all else. He was seated next to his fiancée in the center of the seventh row, looking, or so Louisa thought, totally bored by his surroundings. But then, whenever did he not? she asked herself. Certainly she envied his detachment. For the sight of him had brought on a sudden rush of longing, followed by an even more intense wave of hatred for the Honourable Miss Sedgwick, whose hand was placed so possessively upon his lordship's sleeve. Neither emotion was likely to help her portrayal of Columbine, Louisa realized. Pity they weren't doing tragedy. She'd make a fine Medea at the moment. She smiled wryly at her feeble attempt at humor, then gave up audience-watching altogether. With a great effort of will, Louisa managed to blot the spectators from her mind and began to concentrate upon the gay, irrepressibly mischievous personality of the role she had to play.

For a little while, they almost got away with it. When Louisa skipped upon the stage, there was a spontaneous burst of applause from the male portion of the viewers in tribute to her beauty. Then, for another plus, Louisa and Jem were rather good in the scenes they played together, she decided with that detached section of an actor's mind reserved for observation even while immersed in the business of the play. Jem had all the makings of an actor, she thought proudly as they romped through one of their more boisterous scenes. And she had every right to be proud of him. For just as Kean had raised the level of her Desdemona, so she was lifting Jem's performance now.

But it was not to last. For someone in the audience—the host himself, perhaps—recalled just why this troupe had been engaged and what the real night's entertainment was supposed to be. "Boo!" boomed out a voice, followed by a female titter. "Hiss!" a woman giggled quaveringly, and the audience snickered after her.

Louisa and Jem rose above this interruption, though, and managed to regain the audience's attention. But then their scene was over and other players took the stage. The boos and hisses increased in frequency and volume, as did the laughter from those egging the hecklers on. Louisa made her next appearance just as an orange splattered on the stage. The second one struck her arm. She managed to ignore it and go on.

But there was no hope now of getting the audience back into the play. Heckling the performers was a great deal more entertaining than the antics of Harlequin, Pantaloon, and Columbine could ever be. Louisa gritted her teeth and broadened her characterization. No use. The audience was in an uproar of laughter, calling out insults and peppering the stage with rotten fruit conveniently provided underneath their seats in charming little baskets by their thoughtful host.

When a particularly messy orange splattered

187

Aunt Nell's bosom, followed by shrieks of delighted laughter, Louisa went berserk. She stooped down, scooped up the rotten fruit, and hurled it back with deadly accuracy. Lord Lyston made an easy target. He was already on his feet. The projectile hit him with a sickening squash, exploding in bright orange over his snowy shirtfront and white neckcloth. The Honourable Miss Sedgwick let out a shriek. Then Louisa hit her for good measure.

From that moment on, it was war. Louisa was scooping up oranges and pelting them at the audience indiscriminately, except for intermittent volleys designed to stave off Lord Lyston's inexorable advance and one direct hit on Lady Follett. Jem let out a whoop of exultation and joined in the barrage.

The tide of battle suddenly shifted in the actors' favor. The surprise of their counterattack had caused a panic. The audience was shrieking in terror now, ducking down behind their seats, afraid to run for fear of becoming a marked target. But just as it looked as though they'd be forced to risk it and retreat, two things happened all at once. Lyston leaped the row of candles bordering the stage and landed on it. He ducked Louisa's final orange, flung directly at his face, grabbed her in a flying tackle, threw her across his shoulder, and bore her off, no easy feat as she kicked and screeched out her defiance, both at him and at the audience, while accompanying herself with a tattoo of pounding fists upon his back. As all this was taking place, frantic Farnsworth servants reached the wings and pulled the curtains closed.

Lyston lowered a hysterical Louisa to the floor, where she quickly went on the attack again. Tears streaming down her face, her costume splattered with stinking orange, she hurled herself upon him, kicking, clawing, even biting in her rage. He fended her off as gently as he could at first. "Stop it, Louisa, control yourself. Stop it now, it's over." But when he saw she was too far gone for reason, he shook her hard, which infuriated her all the more. Then he slapped her face. She stared up at him in shock—and softly began to sob.

"Louisa, I'm sorry—truly," he whispered, his face a mirror of the misery he felt. "I didn't want to hurt you. I just didn't know how else to bring you round. I'm sorry. I really am." He reached out to touch her, but she drew away. Her sobs had subsided but the tears continued to trace patterns on her cheeks through her heavy makeup. "I'm sorry," he said again, helplessly.

"It doesn't matter," she replied woodenly. "It's all of a piece, is it not? Bear baitings, rat pits, throwing things at actors."

"For God's sake, Louisa. I had nothing to do with any of this. Besides, I had no idea you'd even be here."

"That I'd be here!" she blazed again. "What difference does that make?" She gestured broadly toward her colleagues, who were making desultory stabs at cleaning up while covertly watching the two combatants. "These are people, too. Did that never occur to you?" Her voice was growing hysterical once more, and his lordship seemed to be weighing the hazards of trying to slap her again when a throat cleared just behind them.

"I say, Lyston, would you present me to your charming companion?"

The two wheeled from glaring at one another to find Lord Faircot leaning heavily upon his silver-topped walking stick and observing them with a great deal of interest.

"He's enjoying this immensely," was his daughter's first impression. And indeed, though his lordship's countenance was entirely sober, his gray eyes could not quite overcome his desire to laugh. "He's aged," was her second thought as she noted the deep lines in the once-handsome face and perceived that, in spite of his herculean efforts to disguise the fact, it was difficult for him to stand. Still, he was very much in control of the situation. "Lyston," he prompted the younger man politely.

His lordship, who seemed at the point of wishing Faircot to the devil, more or less recovered. "Lord Faircot, may I present Mrs. Var—err, that is to say, Miss Grayson." There was hardly a trace of civility in Lord Lyston's tone.

"Grayson?" Lord Faircot inquired. "A relative of yours, perhaps?"

"No. Yes. Damn it, I suppose so."

"A very distant relative, then, I take it, since you appear to be unsure," Faircot remarked dryly. He looked Louisa up and down. "I doubt she's much kin to you. No offense, sir, but no Grayson was ever quite so lovely. The moment the young lady stepped onstage, I was quite bedazzled. Let me offer my congratulations, my dear. Yours was a remarkable performance." Louisa gave him a withering look. "No, no, indeed, I mean it. I frankly did not know which to admire more, your ability as a thespian, which is considerable—I must confess that came as something of a surprise. Have you noticed, Lyston, that the beauties are rarely talented? Don't have to be, I suppose. Oh, well, then." He shrugged as Lyston only glared. "As I was saying"—he focused once more upon Louisa—"much as I admired your acting, I had to admire your marksmanship even more. And may I thank you for not including me in your several targets? I rather expected it, you know. And since you have an unerring habit of hit-ting what you aim for"—he looked pointedly at Lyston's shirtfront—"I anticipated the worst of fates. But others seemed to have a more immediate claim to your hostilities."

He gazed thoughtfully at Lyston for a moment longer before availing himself of Louisa's hand. "I must not keep you. I simply felt I had to thank you for a highly entertaining evening."

"I'm glad you found it so amusing," Louisa said coldly as he kissed her hand lingeringly while Lyston glared.

Lord Faircot by no means overlooked Lyston's hostile gaze. "Fascinating," he murmured to his daughter. "But then I suppose you've always had the power to do just that. I look forward to seeing you again soon, Miss Grayson," he added rather more loudly than necessary, Louisa thought. Faircot threw an amused glance over his shoulder to encounter Lyston's hard, suspicious stare. "In the theater, of course," he qualified. Then, chuckling at some private joke, he left.

With a threat of renewed tears that took her completely by surprise, Louisa watched him go. "I wonder what price he's paid for this little scene," she asked herself, as her father, pausing to speak to Mr. Scopes, leaned more heavily still upon his cane.

"Please don't let me detain you either, Lord Lyston." For all her fruit-splashed costume and raddled makeup, Louisa achieved a quiet dignity. "I would not wish to keep you from your friends. Who knows what other amusements may be planned for your entertainment. You could always set a few man-traps for poachers. And let me see, what else? But then, of course, you already plan to set a pack of dogs on a defenseless little fox and ride it down tomorrow, do you not?"

Lyston stared at her a moment, opened his mouth to speak, then changed his mind and shrugged. "What's the use? You're determined to think me a villain no matter what. As you say, I'd best remove these stinking clothes. You do the same. Good night." Lyston bowed slightly and went striding back on stage. He jumped across the footlights to the floor below, oblivious to the stares of curious servants. "It's the only route he knows, I guess," Louisa thought distractedly.

"I say, Louisa, you were rather rough on him." Jem had been listening shamelessly to the exchange. "He was trying to rescue you, you know, when he came leaping up onstage. But the way you kept rocking him with oranges, you must of thought he'd gone on the attack."

"With Lord Lyston, it's often difficult to tell the difference," Louisa muttered as she turned and walked away toward their makeshift dressing room.

Chapter
Sixteen

FOR EVERYONE BUT LOUISA, THE MOONLIGHT CAR-
riage ride back to Bath was an amazingly cheer-
ful one. What had first appeared to be an economic
disaster had turned into a windfall.

After Sir Peter Farnsworth had done his best to
placate his routed guests, he had appeared backstage breathing fire and brimstone. He had ordered
the actors off his premises and, at the mention of
their payment, had gone off like a rocket. "The fee!"
he screamed at Mr. Scopes. "You've the nerve to ask
for money after attacking my guests like maniacs!
My solicitor will speak to you of fees, sir. Now leave
my house!"

Mr. Scopes had hardly had time for the dismal
realization to sink in that, not only would they not
be getting paid but he was also out the expenses of
the hackney coach, when a servant cleared his
throat at the manager's elbow and whispered,
"Lord Faircot would like a word with you."

"Now, there's a gentleman!" Mr. Scopes's eyes blinked a staccato tribute as he beamed at his fellow passengers. "He told me as how he'd a notion that 'old clutch-fisted Farnsworth'—those were his lordship's very words—wouldn't pay us, and as how he didn't like the idea that we should suffer for the best evening's entertainment he'd had in years. Then he asked what Sir Peter had engaged us for and doubled it. Now, there's a gentleman!"

"A good job nobody pelted him," one of the bit players remarked thankfully.

"No luck about it," Jem remarked. "Who's going to peg away at a man in an invalid chair, I ask you? That's worse than flinging stuff at actors who ain't allowed to throw it back. At least, no actor ever did before. But then they went and got Louisa's dander up!" he crowed. Jem was still savoring the victory in what he forever afterward referred to as "The Battle of Farnsworth Hall." He dwelled at length on this or that particularly good shot he'd made, but most of his admiration was for Louisa, who had "led the charge like a regular Wellington."

While Louisa's face flamed at the memory, Jem described dramatically the moment when she had scooped up her first orange and hurled it. The others laughed themselves into convulsions at his reenactment. Well, she could certainly understand their mirth. It was time that these worms did a bit of turning. Actors lived barely on the edge of suffrance and were constantly being called upon to grovel before obstreperous audiences. It was not at all unusual for a manager or leading man to make an apologetic curtain speech after an audience staged a riot. Thanks to her, their little group had shattered that mold to smithereens. What the repercussions might be, though, heaven only knew. Louisa feared that from now on the Scopeses might find engagements even harder to come by than they had been before. Thank goodness her father had saved them from this night's disaster that she had caused. As for the future—for the moment, it was too painful to contemplate.

Louisa spent what was left of the night in Bath. She shared Aunt Nell's four-poster, trying hard not to shift her position too frequently while she lay wide-eyed, reviewing the nightmare evening time after ghastly time. Just when she was sure Aunt Nell was sound asleep, the bed began to shake. The old lady finally gasped through a fit of laughter, "Who was that Friday-faced female sitting with his lordship?"

"Which lordship?" Louisa asked.

"Don't play games with me, dearie. There's only one lordship where you're concerned. The one that's in love with you."

"He's not in love with me, and that was his fiancée."

"Well then, that explains it."

"Explains what?"

"Why you picked on her, in spite of his lordship already leaping over people's heads to get onstage. Must of thought that diamond pendant 'twixt her tits was a bull's-eye, for you nailed it true to rights. Lord, did she screech! I vow, you really coated that one's cleavage. And good enough for her, waving both her assets in front of his lordship's nose that way. Much good it did her, if you want my opinion. Still, in one way, it probably worked out to her advantage. That dress was so far down toward her navel as not to have been splashed at all, most likely." She choked with laughter.

And then, at the memory of the Honourable Letitia Sedgwick's shrieks, Louisa snickered, too. Soon she was giggling as hard as her companion. "It was an accident," she finally managed to gasp. "I didn't aim for her in particular."

"Oh, didn't you," Aunt Nell retorted. "You can gammon some, miss, but you can't gammon me."

Louisa opened her mouth to protest her innocence of any malice toward Miss Sedgwick, then closed it once again. She thought it best not to explore that particular incident too closely. She feared that Aunt Nell, in her aged wisdom, just might be right.

Over breakfast the next morning Louisa and the Scopeses made a few halfhearted plans for their next production. They spoke with forced optimism of the bookings they were sure to get. All the euphoria of the night before had vanished. They were hard put not to show their anxiety for the future.

But at that, breakfast was the high point of Louisa's day. She returned to the Dower House to spend the afternoon peeping out her window for signs of activity in the Hall. For she had learned from Joe that his lordship was in residence and "things were on their ear up there, him being cross as a bear and in a taking the likes of which his staff had never seen." But if Louisa hoped for a glimpse of Graylands' lord and master, she was doomed to disappointment. She went to bed that evening in a mood of dark despair. Certainly Lyston would wish never to see her again. She now recalled the Battle of Farnsworth Hall with a shudder.

But when Katie poked her head in the bedchamber next day and said, "A gentleman's here to pay a morning call, miss," Louisa had raced halfway down the stairs before realizing that Katie would hardly announce Lord Lyston in such a way.

So she was not as surprised as she otherwise

might have been to find her father waiting in the drawing room.

"Forgive me for not rising." He was seated in his invalid chair again. "I can, but it's an effort I'd as soon forgo."

Louisa looked at her parent suspiciously while amusement flickered on his face. From his attitude, they might have been on the closest terms. It took some effort to remind herself that he'd disowned her in a rage some years before.

"I've never understood you at all," she blurted.

"Good," he answered. "It feeds my vanity to be considered an enigma, whereas in reality I'm rather a simple sort of man. But do sit down, my dear. I'm getting a crick in my neck from looking up at you."

Feeling rather like the little girl she used to be, Louisa obediently sat down on a black-and-gold japanned armchair opposite her father. "That's better," he said amiably. "Much more conducive to a comfortable coze." Then he laughed as she glared at him.

"Well, my dear," he picked up the conversational thread once more, "you say you've never understood me. And I, your father, don't know you at all. I've come to think that's quite a tragedy, especially after your impressive performance at Farnsworth Hall." He chuckled at the memory.

"It was good of you to pay Mr. Scopes." It cost Louisa a bit to say so, which her father seemed to appreciate, judging by the increased twinkle in his eye. "The company desperately needs the money Lord Farnsworth had promised them."

"Yes, I expected that they might. As I told your Mr. Scopes, it was little enough to do for the most fun I've had in years." He lapsed into silence as Katie came into the room carrying a tea board.

Louisa smiled her appreciation for the hospitality she'd been too agitated to think of.

"A very nice room, this," Lord Faircot remarked as Katie left. Louisa poured tea for both of them and passed him bread and butter. "You do seem to have landed on your feet. Tell me, are you Lyston's mistress?"

Louisa choked on the tea that she was sipping. "Indeed, I am not!" She glared when she'd recovered.

"No? Well, no need to get up on your high ropes about it. I'd prefer it to your being Varley's wife. But by the by, I understand you weren't that, either."

"You seem remarkably well-informed," she retorted icily.

"Indeed, I'm not. I feel completely in the dark in fact." He gazed around the room pointedly. "But yes, word did get back to me that Varley, in addition to being a toad-eater, a fortune hunter, and an ass, was also a bigamist. I then tried to send a servant to Brussels to fetch you home." Her eyebrows shot up in disbelief and he smiled wryly. "Come now, Louisa, no matter what you choose to think of me, you've little cause to doubt my word." She acknowledged the truth of that, and he continued. "At any rate, Napoleon had gone on his rampage, then, and by the time Yates made it to Brussels, you'd disappeared. No one had the slightest idea what had become of you in all the uproar. And since I kept on looking for a Mrs. Varley—or a Miss Faircot—it's little wonder I had no success in finding you. For here you are, a Mrs. Grayson. I do hope you intend explaining that, at least," he said in his customary detached mode of speaking. "Really, I'm quite agog."

"It's a rather long story," Louisa said with reluctance.

"I can wait."

"The thing is, I was—in a manner of speaking—married to Adrian Grayson, Lord Lyston's brother."

"Gracious! Your marriages all seem to have a habit of being 'in a manner of speaking,' do they not? Oh, I beg your pardon, m'dear," he said quickly as she seemed about to rise and terminate their conversation. "That was a caddish thing to say. And here I've been lecturing myself repeatedly not to indulge in any 'I told you so's' about Nicholas Varley. It doesn't appear I'm going to comply with my better instincts, does it?"

"Did you ever?" Louisa asked nastily.

"No, I suppose not. But do go on, m'dear. About your—er—'marriage' to Lyston's brother."

"I'd known Adrian for ages." Louisa's reluctance was evident, but she forced herself to give her father a brief account. "He had wanted to marry me, which I had said was out of the question. Then he was wounded at Quatre Bras—and dying." In spite of herself, tears came into Louisa's eyes. "And he had the obsession that if we married, it would put things right for me, make me respectable again after the coil Varley had left me in. And so we went through a ceremony. I don't know if it was even legal. Lyston says it was not." Her father's brows rose again. "My solicitor does not agree. I hadn't really cared one way or another until there was an incident in London—but I'd rather not go into all that right now."

"A pity," Lord Faircot murmured.

"Anyhow, I was angry at Lyston's attitude. I needed a place to stay, and I thought I'd show him he didn't rule the world. So I took possession of this house. Did I say that it was Adrian's? And here I am."

"I see." Her father made it obvious by his tone

that he did not see at all. After a pause, he inquired politely, "And I suppose Lord Lyston is also in love with you?"

"Of course not."

"I see nothing 'of course' about it. I'd think any red-blooded man—and Lyston strikes me as all of that—who was in your presence for a full ten seconds would succumb. But perhaps I'm prejudiced. Still, your record would seem to bear me out."

"Lord Lyston is betrothed."

"Oh, no, that he is not." Lord Faircot held up his hand as his daughter started to correct him. "I assure you I am not mistaken. It was the *on dit* of Farnsworth Hall. Indeed, that prosy old bore Sir Peter will never top this party for social success if he lives beyond Methuselah. People will be talking of it for years to come. The theater riot would have assured it immortality. But believe me, the Sedgwick-Lyston set-to was at least as good. Bluebloods, you understand. That's always better value for the gossip-mongers than you hoi-polloi players can expect to be." He smiled.

"What on earth are you talking about?"

"Just that the Honourable Letitia Sedgwick had the noisy hysterics after you struck her with the orange. A very good shot, m'dear—but then I've already complimented you on your marksmanship. At any rate, afterward she cornered Lyston in his room. She was too enraged, evidently, to stop herself from tying her garters in public as it were, for the scene could be heard all up and down the hall. At least it could if one left the door ajar in order not to miss a word of it, as I can testify." He chuckled.

"At any rate, it's my opinion that Lyston has real cause to be grateful to you for bringing Miss Sedgwick's true character out into the open. Otherwise he might not have realized till after the marriage that she's a regular termagant. I don't care how plump in the pocket her father is. Lyston's well rid of her, I can tell you."

"You mean she's broken their engagement?"

"Yes, along with a few of the Farnsworth *objets d'art* from the sound of it. She had a full-blown screaming tantrum. By the by, I suppose that's where I got the mistaken idea that Lyston's in love with you. The Honourable Miss Sedgwick seems to be laboring under the same misapprehension. At least she accused him of it at the very top of her lung power."

"She did?" Louisa gasped as her eyes grew wider.

"Oh, yes," her father answered, then paused a bit. "Unfortunately, though I certainly pricked up my ears, you understand, I could not hear his comeback. Indeed, his entire part in the episode remains a mystery since he was the calmer of the two. But have no fear," he added mischievously, "I'm sure he denied it just as you have."

"Well, now, m'dear." He hauled himself up out of his invalid chair with great difficulty, using his stick for leverage. "That damned quack I see says I must practice walking a bit each hour to get my circulation going. I'll do my constitutional now by fetching Frederick instead of ringing for him. No doubt he's with your servants swilling tea. This will give me an opportunity to see the house you've confiscated. If you could spare an arm, Louisa." As he leaned heavily upon her, they took a few halting steps toward the mantel in order that Lord Faircot might inspect a pair of shepherd-and-shepherdess figurines. "Charming," he murmured, then shifted his attention to Louisa. Tilting her face up toward him, he studied it in much the same way as he had the figurines. "Are you happy, m'dear?" he finally asked.

"Happy?" Louisa repeated. "It's a word I've ceased to think much about. But I am making a life for myself."

"You must know why I'm here, Louisa," he said almost gruffly. "I want you to come and live with me."

"Take your hands off her, you filthy lecher!" Lord Lyston was standing in the doorway, his face livid, his hands clenched into fists. He was all but breathing fire.

As he took a menacing step in their direction, Lord Faircot put an arm around Louisa's shoulders. "Do you think I should climb back into my invalid chair?" he asked casually. "Surely he would not strike a cripple. Still, one can never be sure with these sporting types. And this one looks like one of Gentleman Jackson's protégés. Am I not right?" He addressed that question to Lyston with remarkable detachment considering the fact that the other was advancing menacingly.

"You're right that I'll not strike you. But I *will* throw you out of here. Take your hands off Mrs. Grayson."

"And what right have you to make that demand, sir? None at all, so I've been given to understand."

"By whom?"

"Why, by Mrs. Grayson. She has just assured me that you care nothing for her."

"If she said that, she's a cursed liar." Lyston glared in her direction.

"Not very gallantly put, but I do take your drift. Still, though, I think you must admit that I can do a great deal more for the little minx than you can." Lord Faircot was obviously enjoying the situation immensely. Louisa was toying with the idea of hit-ting him herself. She settled for a dirty look instead. "I don't like to boast, my dear Lyston," her father went on to say, "but plump in the pocket as you undoubtedly are, your fortune can't begin to measure up to mine. And I intend to make Louisa my sole heir. As you surely have observed, I can't last forever. Now can you top that, I ask you?"

"I can, if loving her and making her my wife counts for anything."

Louisa stared at first in disbelief, then thought it high time she entered the conversation. "Loving me? You never mentioned loving me."

"The devil I did not! Why else would I have been asking you to marry me, for God's sake?"

"You most certainly never mentioned that you loved me!"

"Well, I do. So you'll damned well have to make a choice now, won't you? Me or this overaged lecher and his promised inheritance, which you'd be a fool to count on. Choose, Louisa."

"Oh, I don't think she'll have to be quite so dramatic. Louisa, do push my chair over here. I'm finding this Cheltenham tragedy to be entertaining, but also rather wearing." Louisa complied with her father's request, and he sank down upon the seat and sighed gratefully.

Lyston stared at him. "Surely, Louisa, you can't seriously consider—look at the man—it's obscene. He needs a nurse, not a mistress."

"Oh, I don't know," Lord Faircot mused. "I've had scores of nurses in the past few years and not a single mistress. Might be just the thing."

Lord Lyston took another menacing step forward while Louisa snapped, "Oh, Father, stop it!"

"Father!" Lyston halted, as though he'd just been pole-axed.

"Of course 'Father,'" Lord Faircot said pleasantly. "Surely you were not thinking otherwise?"

"But I don't understand." Lyston was looking dazed. He stared at Louisa uncomprehendingly. "You mean you are his natural daughter?"

"I must say, Lyston," Lord Faircot spoke up dryly, "your mind does seem to be overly inclined to take the low road. Louisa is definitely not some by-blow of mine gotten on the parlormaid. She is legally as well as morally my daughter. My only child, in fact. And, to be frank about it, she has been quite sufficient."

Lord Lyston, who had grown alarmingly still and even more pale than previously, continued to stare at Louisa a few minutes longer. "Well, Miss Faircot," he said when he finally found his voice, "I'm sure you've derived much amusement at my expense from your charade. Now, if you'll excuse me." He bowed woodenly in her direction, and, with a curt nod toward her father, left the room.

Chapter
Seventeen

*L*OUISA SPENT THE NEXT SEVERAL HOURS WONDERING what to do. Katie settled the matter for her. "Did you know, ma'am," she inquired the morning after Lyston's confrontation with Louisa's father, "that his lordship plans to leave for London tomorrow morning? He'll be taking up residence there again, they say." There was nothing subtle about Katie's approach, but her mistress was grateful for it.

It was unusual for Louisa to lavish so much time upon her toilette. She changed her gown three times, then settled on the one she'd put on first: a lilac merino walking dress which she persuaded herself would deepen the color of her eyes.

The weather was not cooperative to her venture. She sighed at the blowing rain that made pattens and an umbrella necessary. And by the time she had trudged across the park and up the hill, the coiffure she'd toiled so long upon was completely disarrayed. In fact—she sighed as she rang the bell—she was a sodden mess.

"Would you tell Lord Lyston," she instructed an astonished butler, "that Miss Faircot has come to tea?"

"Do come in, miss." The august presence ushered her into the entrance hall, where he relieved her of her dripping cloak. Louisa gazed around inquisitively. The focal point of interest was the staircase that fanned out in two directions from the center of the hall to meet again and form a gallery above. Rows of ornately framed Grayson ancestors marched above the staircase rails and along the gallery. They stared woodenly before them, for the most part, although occasionally some exceptional talent had contrived to give a portrait life. Most of Lord Lyston's ancestors looked decidedly forbidding, Louisa thought. One exception, near her above the stairs, was a smiling young man dressed in the costume of the previous century, who looked amazingly like Adrian.

"The best fire's in the library, miss." The butler was obviously concerned about her dampness. "Come this way, please. I'll inform his lordship of your arrival."

Louisa toasted herself gratefully before the roaring fire. Indeed, she was quite dry, had put her hair in order, and was beginning to think that Lord Lyston had refused to see her before he finally appeared. His looks were not exactly prepossessing, she noted clinically. The fault was certainly not with his superbly tailored coat of dark blue superfine, or his biscuit pantaloons and gleaming hessians. It lay in his haggard face and jaundiced stare. If he was not suffering the ill effects of a bout of drinking, Louisa missed her guess.

They stood and waited while the butler laid out

the tea things. "It's Miss Faircot today, is it?" Lord Lyston asked politely when they were finally alone.

Louisa shrugged. "It is difficult to choose among so many names. But I suppose I have the greatest claim to being Faircot. At least I have now, after seeing my father yesterday. It was questionable before."

Lyston nodded curtly toward the tea things, and Louisa seated herself at the Pembroke table and poured tea for both of them. "You certainly took your time in coming just now," she remarked conversationally. "I had decided you did not wish to see me."

"How could you ever think that?" Lyston asked sarcastically. "Once you've been removed from my life for good, I don't know what I shall do for amusement. Not to mention mystery and drama. The delay was simply that I had not shaved. I did not wish to encounter the famed Faircot beauty looking so disreputable."

"I'm glad of that," Louisa replied candidly while handing him a seed cake, which he ignored. "For I must say you look rather hag-ridden, as it is."

"Thank you. Are you surprised that I came home from that charming scene with you and your long-lost father and got a trifle drunk?"

"No," Louisa retorted, "I'm not surprised. But it was a caper-witted thing to do."

"Perhaps. But it's one reaction—and a fairly natural one—to having been made a fool of for all these months. Tell me, did you enjoy your masquerade?"

"It was no masquerade." The interview was not going as she'd planned. But then, her encounters with Lord Lyston never did, Louisa thought despondently. They always arrived eventually at drawn daggers. "When my father disowned me for eloping, I refused to be forever dropping my maiden name to impress whatever snobs I happened to run into." Lyston bridled at her terminology, but bit back his comment. "Knowing I was a Faircot might have made you a bit less prejudiced, Lord Lyston. But be honest, please. Would it have helped so very much? You were determined to think the worst of me."

"Of course it would have helped—oh, how the devil would I know? After what Lady Follett told me—"

"She told you essentially the truth." Louisa put her cup down carefully. Her hand was trembling just a bit. "I had been living for six years with a man who was not my husband. You see, I eloped when I was but seventeen. My father, who possessed a lot more insight into Nicholas Varley's character than into mine, spotted Nicholas for a scheming fortune hunter and forbade me to see him. I was always more stubborn than discerning"—Lyston almost smiled at that, she saw—"so I regarded my father's ultimatum as a gauntlet flung down to be picked up. I ran off to Gretna Green with Varley. It did not take me long to discover that my father had been right—a painful habit of his where I was concerned. It's very hard to forgive someone for always being right, you know. But it took much longer to discover that Varley had a wife—and oh, yes"—her face contorted painfully—"a child as well. At least I was spared that." She could not look at Lyston now. "I had been living as Varley's wife for only a few months when I discovered that he was incapable of being faithful. Our marriage after that was only pretense. And I will say this for Varley: he never tried to force me. But perhaps that was no hardship on his part. It had been my fortune which had attracted him. And, as I said, he had interests elsewhere."

"My God!" Lyston breathed.

"Anyhow," Louisa rallied and continued, "it was eventually discovered that Varley was a bigamist, he was cashiered, and I found myself a fallen woman, ostracized by all my erstwhile friends."

Louisa made herself look at Lyston then and found the pain in his face harder to bear than his hostility. "Except for Adrian," he said.

"Yes, Adrian. That's why I've forced myself upon your time this way. Partly why, at any rate," she qualified. "I want to explain to you about Adrian. I think it's important that you know." She held up her hand to stop his protest. "Whatever becomes of you and me, and we do seem to have made a mess of things, I'm determined that you should realize that we do have one bond between us. We both loved Adrian." Then, as she saw him wince, she added deliberately, "Like a brother.

"He and I had been friends since he first joined the regiment. I didn't realize it for a long, long while, but with him the friendship took on another character. He fancied himself in love with me."

"I'm sure it was more than a fancy," Adrian's brother said.

"Perhaps you're right. At first I simply looked on it as a young boy's calf-love. You know, the usual thing, mooning over someone who is older, unattainable. Perhaps that's all it ever would have been. But then Varley was cashiered, and Adrian was terribly concerned about me." Louisa's eyes filled with tears. "And he was determined to set things right by marrying me.

"Please believe me now. I had no intention of ever doing so. I was not deliberately deceiving you at the Duchess of Richmond's ball." She looked at

209

Lyston imploringly. "I knew I'd be taking advantage of his youth and inexperience. I had found a position with the Scopeses and was quite determined to be an actress. I felt I could support myself by acting. Adrian disapproved, of course, and urged me all the more to be his wife. But I kept refusing his proposals. When he asked me to go to the Duchess's ball with him, I refused that, too, at first. Then I decided it might be a good idea for him to see firsthand what a leper I'd become." Lyston's face contorted as he recalled the part he'd played that night in her humiliation, but he did not speak. "Well, he saw, all right. But I fear my scheme had a reverse effect. He was more determined than ever to put me under his protection."

"Yes, he would have been." Lyston was staring into his cup, intent as a tea-leaf reader, unable to look at her.

"Then—well, you know what happened. Wellington was there. News came of the French advance. Suddenly it was as if the world would spin right off its axis. We left the ball. I had the coachman drive him home. And—I fear you may think even less of me for this part," she said in a low voice. "When he was leaving me, he implored me again to marry him. He said he didn't think he could face what was coming unless I agreed to—and, well—I told him that I would."

A muscle twitched in Lord Lyston's cheek. Otherwise he was still as death, Louisa noted as she continued. "It was perhaps a cowardly thing I did—as well as a dishonorable one—but I don't suppose I would do differently again. It was all so horrible—what he was about to face—that I felt I had to do anything within my power to help him. I felt that when it was all over, I could tell him gently that it would never do. But of course that was not the way it was to be."

Louisa dabbed ineffectually at her eyes with her fingertips, and Lyston handed her his handkerchief. She accepted it with gratitude but wondered if he might not need it soon himself.

"Anyhow, Adrian was obsessed with the idea that he must rescue me. And he clung to the notion when he was hurt so badly. Webster said he only stayed alive by sheer willpower until the thing was done. Even if I had wanted to back out then—which seemed unthinkable—I believe Webster would have held a gun to my head until the ceremony could be performed." Louisa had tried to speak jokingly, but it fell quite flat. Lyston looked as though he were now present at his brother's deathbed.

"And I still do not know whether I was married legally or not." Louisa attempted to pull him back to the present by speaking as matter-of-factly as she could. "As my father pointed out, I seem destined always to be vague upon that point. Richard, please, please don't continue to look like that." She startled herself at her free use of his first name, but he apparently never noticed. He turned a tortured face to look at her.

"Why could you not have told me all this before?"

"I don't know," Louisa answered miserably. "I'm quite proud, you know. And you thought so little of me. Besides, I never believed you would accept my version of the truth. And I simply could not bring myself to plead my own defense. As I've said, I *am* quite proud," she finished lamely.

"Well!" Lyston's voice was bitter. "I did it all up brown, did I not—'fortune hunter,' 'light-skirt'—I didn't leave out much."

"You did omit 'bigamist.' Still, that was Varley's

211

title, not really mine. 'Partner in bigamy,' perhaps?"

"Stop it, Louisa. You don't have to rub it in. I really don't believe I could think much lower of myself. If I have any excuse, it was that when Adrian was killed, I went through hell. He was more like a son to me, I think, than like a brother. I'd almost raised him, after all. And I should have held firm. I should never have permitted him to join the army."

"We have discussed all this before," Louisa said gently. "You could not have prevented it."

He gave her a grateful look. "Anyhow, I saw you as just one more thing from which I should have saved my little brother. That was easier, I suppose, than directing all my bitterness toward myself."

"And I don't imagine Lady Follett painted a glowing picture of me either." Louisa wrinkled up her nose distastefully. "By the by, I don't like that woman above half. She behaved despicably to Webster."

"She's a—" His lordship's choice of words sent Louisa's brows up to her hairline, but she giggled and he managed an answering grin. "That's one of the smaller ironies of this coil," he went on to say. "In all the years she's been my neighbor, I'd never before given the slightest credence to any of her gossip-mongering. And why I swallowed her version of this affair completely defies all reason."

"You wished to, I expect."

"Yes, I suppose so," he said morosely. "And of course when I saw you for the first time—even in that godawful production in the Brussels opera house—I could believe anything along those lines to be the gospel truth."

"Thank you very much." Louisa glared.

"You do possess a looking glass, do you not?

You're certainly typecast to lure young men into folly. I'm hardly a green 'un—or at least I used to think not," he added ruefully, "but one look at you and I was a goner."

"If you were, you certainly hid it well."

"I didn't hide it at all. For when it comes right down to it, I'm sure that accounts more for my shatter-brained behavior than anything. Here I was, supposedly set to rescue my brother from the clutches of a temptress, and after one look, I was fully as taken in as he."

"You poor thing!" Louisa said with heavy sarcasm.

"Yes, I was rather pathetic, was I not?"

They sat in silence for a bit. Then Louisa stood.

"You're going?" Lord Lyston looked dismayed, but rose politely.

"Oh, no. I'd just like to see the house now, please."

"You mean you'd like a tour?" He obviously thought she'd parted company with her wits.

"Will you take me through it?" she inquired impatiently. "Or shall I ring for your butler and ask him to do it?"

"No, I'll play guide," he said ungraciously. "Though why you want to see it is more than I can understand. It's hardly a showplace."

"I know," Louisa replied mischievously. "When I first rode out here and you asked me in your most haughty tone if I was properly impressed by it, I quite longed to tell you that the house I grew up in in Yorkshire is by far its architectural superior."

He sighed heavily as they started toward the door. "Well, that's one. I was wondering how long it would take for you to begin hurling my words back into my teeth. I can hardly wait till you get to my offer of *carte blanche*."

"Oh, I have several juicy bits to dispose of before

I get to that." She laughed. "Besides," she added seriously, "I don't recall that scene with much pleasure either. You see, I was naïve enough at first to think you actually intended marriage. That gave my pride another blow, I fear."

It was obvious that he wished to change the subject. "Come on," he said gruffly, "since you're determined to be a tourist."

But as a tour guide, Lord Lyston left a great deal to be desired. He was rather prone to whisk Louisa through all the rooms, waiting impatiently if she paused to look more particularly at a piece of furniture or inspect a painting. This did not happen often, though, for she seemed content for the most part to generally acquaint herself with the house's floor plan. Even so, it took quite a while to make their rounds. Lyston was obviously relieved when they finally arrived back in his library.

"Well—satisfied?" he asked.

"No, not really," Louisa answered candidly. "I thought at first the solarium might be converted, but I doubt it would be satisfactory. All in all, I think the only solution is for you to add a wing."

There was no doubt now he thought she'd come unhinged. "Why the devil should I do that?"

"To house a theater, of course."

"A theater! Why in God's name should I add a theater?"

"Well, it's unreasonable to expect me to give up the stage entirely," Louisa said as she began wandering around the room, studiously reading the titles on the shelves. "You yourself finally admitted, after all those odious things you said at first, that I'm actually a rather accomplished actress. Besides," she added, her face looking stormy, "I want a place for people like the Scopeses—well, all right, then, for the Scopeses in particular—to perform

214

where they'll not be degraded. And really, I think you'd come in time to like theatricals. You'll probably wish to act in them yourself."

Lyston snorted. "That will be the day! But you still have not said just why I'm to build the Scopeses a theater. If it's to be a penance for the bad behavior of my friends at Farnsworth Hall, I assure you I had nothing to do with that. I've never thrown anything at an actor in my life—you have my word on it. Though right now I'm rather tempted." He gave her a pointed look.

"You aren't going to make any of this easy, are you? My father warned me that you would not."

"Louisa, stop it!" He walked over and leaned against the mantelpiece with his arms folded across his chest and glared at her. "Leave your literary cataloging for later, can't you, and tell me what part you're playing now." His face resumed its bitter lines. "You've been in so damned many roles since I've met you that I've lost track. But this is a new one. Are you going to tell me what it's all about?"

Louisa wheeled to face him. "It's about my father. Rather it's *because* of my father. Do you know what makes him so insufferable, why we clashed so often?" The question was obviously rhetorical, so he merely shrugged. "His odious habit of being always right! There is nothing quite so lowering as being around someone who is always right. But after my disastrous experience with Varley, I am determined to take seriously what he has to say, even if it destroys me. Especially where his opinions of his own sex are concerned. And well, yesterday when you stormed out of the house—all right, then, when you left upon your dignity, if you prefer—and I had told him a bit about our past dealings with one another—I do wish you wouldn't look quite so mur-

215

derous. You did ask me to explain myself. At any rate, he told me that I'd done the unpardonable. I'd made you feel ridiculous. And that you'd forgive murder, infidelity—you name it—before you'd forgive me that. Was he right?"

"Is there some point to all of this? I'm not exactly in the mood for being quizzed."

"Of course there's a point," Louisa answered hotly. "Father said you'd not ask me to marry you again for all the tea in China. Was he right?"

"Well, Miss Faircot, after all those times you read me my character when I tried, you could hardly—"

"There!" Louisa interrupted, looking utterly disgusted. "You see, I knew it. Now perhaps you can understand why my father is so difficult to live with. Well, he said I'd have to be the one to do it."

"Do what?" Lord Lyston was beginning to look confused again.

"Propose to you, of course. Or would it be all right just to say that I accept the offer you made before?"

"I wouldn't think so," he answered, "for my proposal certainly made you furious at the time, which, frankly, I was hard put to understand. Admittedly, it lacked grace and polish. But I saw no reason for it to raise your hackles to the extent it did. And wouldn't it be even less acceptable now that I know you're the daughter of the Great Lord Faircot—with that nonpareil mansion tucked away up North?" He genuflected mockingly.

"No, it definitely would not be. Oh, I don't mean because of that. Whose daughter I am has nothing to say to anything. What changes the situation is that you did finally get around to the truly important part when you were trying to save me from the clutches of that 'dirty old lecher.'" Louisa giggled and he glared.

"That's twice," he said.

"As I was saying, you finally did admit you loved me. Now, if you had said so in the first place—"

"But I did."

"You most assuredly did not."

"I beg to differ. Well, all right, then, perhaps not in so many words. But not to put too fine a point on it, why in the devil would I have been prepared to make a complete cake of myself in the eyes of the world—don't get on your high ropes. Given what I believed about you, the world would have considered me completely addlepated and you know it. As I was saying, why else would I have acted like a complete widgeon if I did not love you?"

"Lust," she said.

"That, too, of course. But I don't think the word quite covers my situation. Though God knows, for a long time there I hoped so."

"It's perfectly obvious"—Louisa sighed—"that you are a complete flat when it comes to making a proper proposal." Louisa stopped abruptly and gave him an assessing look. "But that can't be so. Just what did you say to the Honourable Letitia Sedgwick? You seem to have managed that creditably enough. Never mind," she said hastily as he looked rather dangerous. "You don't have to tell me if you don't wish it. Let's just say that I don't bring out the best in you in that department. But then you don't inspire me, either. Frankly, the thought of going down on one knee to you—figuratively, of course—and having you throw it in my teeth forever afterward is rather galling. But if I must, I must. There is one more thing to settle, though. Before I get on with it, and risk the humiliation of a refusal, do you think, given your considerable pride and all, that you could possibly contrive to live with the skeleton of Varley in your cupboard?"

Lyston's face set grimly. "The only thing about Varley that bothers me is that I may swing for murder if I ever meet him."

"He is not worth it, I assure you," Louisa answered lightly, looking very relieved and grateful all the same.

"But back to that proposal thing. My father did say that if it did not work out—and I am having difficulty in coming up to scratch—there was another way. And on the whole, I think it might be the best."

"Yes, and what was that?" Though he continued to lean against the mantelpiece with folded arms, Lord Lyston's gaze was wary.

"Well"—Louisa began walking toward him slowly—"he did suggest that if all else failed, I most likely could succeed in seducing you. Then he promised to play the outraged father to the hilt and make you marry me."

"And you actually consider yourself capable of carrying out your part of the scheme?" He raised an eyebrow and looked skeptical.

"Oh, yes, I should think so. Given your admitted lust and all."

"But that was then."

"All I can do is try." Louisa came a few steps nearer and smiled up at him. His gaze refused to soften. She laid her palm gently on his cheek. His blue eyes burned into hers, but he made no move. She stood on tiptoe and brushed her lips lightly against his rigid mouth. He did not respond. She stepped back and looked up at him speculatingly. "You are determined to be difficult, aren't you? Well, we'll see." She tried the kiss again, first tantalizing his lips gently with her tongue, then throwing herself more wholeheartedly into the role of his seductress.

The results were electrifying. Lord Lyston's arms came unfolded, and he clasped her to him with rib-crushing strength. She gasped as his lips bruised her own with the force of the passion he'd been holding back. It was a long while before Louisa finally managed to pull herself away.

"Considering your original lack of enthusiasm for my scheme," she gasped, "you've certainly grown cooperative. Maybe a bit too willing, I might point out."

"We've hardly started." He grinned back. "This surely is not your idea of a seduction. Your father will never be able to get me to the altar on just that."

"I'm sorry," Louisa said demurely, "but it will have to do. I've changed my mind about that part. Could we not simply just pretend that you've proposed and I've accepted?"

"Consider it done. All right then, where were we?" He bent his head to kiss her, but she held up a restraining hand.

"I really must insist that you hold your lust in check till after the nuptials, sir, for it occurs to me that I should make it plain I'm not the light-skirt you always took me for."

"A pity that," he murmured, "but it's not too late to rectify the matter. Come here, Louisa." And he reached out and pulled her back into his arms.